SEX EXCURSIONIST

volume 1

Cherries, Love, and Line crossing in Angeles City, Philippines

NATHAN RENLY

Renly Publishing
www.nathanrenly.com

SEX EXCURSIONIST novels are published by

Renly Publishing

ISBN: 9781973519614

Contents

Sex ~~Tourist~~ Excursionist

Sex Excursionist. That's what I am, because that is the title I chose for myself. While it is sure not to confuse anyone, it speaks better than Sex Tourist, and I don't really go on tours anymore. Now, I take excursions to find the sex and companionship that I crave and cannot manage at home. And of course, the Internet address was available.

While the narrator, characters, and events in this story are based in various degrees on the author's experiences (sometimes verbatim), this book is considered a work of fiction. That said, great care was taken to tell an authentic story based on the culture of Angeles City, Philippines, sex workers, and their sex tourist partners.

CHAPTER 1

Touchdowns in Manila

After a 24-hour journey across the Pacific, one I'd completed numerous times in my adult life, I was finally on the ground in Manila, Philippines. I wasn't on business, I wasn't sightseeing, I was on a very specific mission, and I didn't pretend otherwise. I had the moment planned meticulously in my mind, using it as a dream to escape the monotonous grind of an American life. I didn't know yet whether the first night's experience would live up to those lofty fantasies, but the anticipation combined with the jet lag and culture shock was enough to heighten my senses and memory. I remember the first night of a sex vacation as if it were a life-changing event.

My destination was the booming area of Pasay near the Mall of Asia, Resorts World Casino, and the multiplying skeletons of high-end hotel and condo developments, though I wasn't planning to avail myself of any of those new luxuries. I was bound for an area of Pasay that hasn't changed much for decades. Near the intersection of Roxas Blvd and EDSA Ave stands many aging structures including an unassuming strip mall appropriately titled "EDSA International Entertainment Complex" which Filipinos refer to as "EDSA Complex." It is an appropriate name because there exists a tremendous amount of entertainment to be had and only international visitors can really afford it.

Around the area of EDSA Complex stand numerous hotels of various quality most of which offer short time rates. I was bound for the Victoria Court which I had never stayed at but seemed to fit my current budget and accommodation preferences. I had a bit more money to spend this trip so I intended to splurge on better rooms and meals. The Victoria Court was a type of motel that is quite popular in the Philippines. Many of the rooms have their own garage where the discreet couple can pull in privately and do their business, and the hotel's black and white logo of a woman holding her finger over her mouth made no secret as to the typical clientele.

After a short cab ride from the airport, I approached the front desk around 10pm to find a charming young girl with full red lips and a welcoming smile greet me with that distinct Philippine accent I had come to love on my previous trips. I was immediately attracted to her — a result of repressed feelings and desires for too long.

Always look at the room before booking a new hotel in the Philippines.

"I'd like a room for 12 hours please," I said with no shame whatsoever. In fact, I'm certain I was sporting a Joker smile that probably looked ridiculous as if I was a child ready to board Space Mountain.

"We only have one room now for 2,400 pesos," she answered a prepared response.

"Ok, I guess I'll take it."

Based on the Internet, I had expected to get a rate much lower than that, in the 1,300-1,600 range, but I didn't feel like traipsing around Pasay looking for a better deal for the night. I was so eager to make my way to EDSA Complex that I didn't even bother to look at the room first, which is my rule for staying in new Filipino hotels. Always look at the room before booking a new hotel in the Philippines.

"The room comes with breakfast for two starting at six, please ring the front desk when you are ready," she mentioned still smiling.

"For two? Are you going to have breakfast with me?"

I flirted with all the charm I could muster.

She responded with the quintessential Philippine girl giggle with a slight eye roll and no response when a foreigner says something completely inappropriate, and I reminded myself that not every woman in the Philippines wanted to fuck me, in fact, most of them probably didn't. Just 24 hours ago back home in America, if I had made a remark like that, I'm sure it would have been received with a more hostile response.

I was happy to be away from the slightly embarrassing moment and heading towards the room with one of the male attendants, and quickly forgetting my first crush of the trip. It was eerily silent at Victoria Court that night. The hotel reminded me of an American townhouse apartment complex with garages on the bottom floor and units placed on top. There seemed to be no lights on in any of the rooms... *only one room available my ass.* Besides us, there was only a lone security guard slouching on a chair near the gate.

The attendant showed me to an open garage and explained how to open and close the door. Inside, he led me up a staircase to a small foyer with a shelf for placing breakfast in front of the door to the room. Inside, I found a tastefully decorated room with wooden panels holding large mirrors that screamed sex from the pink condom placed on a white towel laid on the white sheets to the tiled easy-to-clean floors. The furniture, TV, and bedding all seemed of higher quality than I was expecting, probably indicative of the higher price.

The attendant showed me around the room a bit and turned on the TV and flipped a few channels indicating the foreign stations.

"Where's the porn?" I asked bluntly. *Why would I give a shit about CNN?*

I'm sure he didn't get that direct question too often, but he nevertheless and somewhat uncomfortably flipped

4

straight to a channel with American porn barely visible through static. *What a total letdown*, I thought and ushered him out the door. I was more curious than anything about the porn. From my visits to Tijuana and the Hotel Cascades, I was used to vivid hardcore porn showing on the TVs in the room where I took a girl for 30 minutes. The porn there seemed necessary to heighten the excitement of the surgical style paid sexual encounter. In the Philippines, however, I didn't need the porn, as there was never a 30-minute time limit and the girls acted more like girlfriends than sex workers.

The quiet in the room when I found myself finally alone after a day of traveling caused a shock of exhaustion and I crashed onto the bed and ended up staring at myself in the mirrors on the ceiling. "Look at you, do you seriously expect any of these girls to be attracted to you?" was the thought I directed at the 45-year-old barely average looking pale American man staring down at me from the crystal-clear glass. The hair had finally started to recede in the last few years at a furious pace and I didn't want to recognize myself, but I knew who it was – a middle aged man who never found satisfaction in his desires, always lacked self-confidence with women, but later in life lost the shame of seeking those desires through whatever means available.

I was still searching. It was likely an endless search, like a drug addict forever seeking that first high.

I wiped the gloom away from my face, chastised myself for the negative thoughts and remembered that pure bliss was less than an hour away. It would be amazing, as it always is. Being in the arms of a beautiful woman was the fix I needed. *And my dick inside of her of course.*

I quickly showered off the stench of 24-hours of travel and headed out the door towards EDSA Complex. Walking past the security guard, I nodded a hello that was received with a wide smile and a "good evening sir!" and emerging onto the streets of Pasay, the culture shock that lessens with every trip but never ceases to meet me on arrival settled in. The nervousness around Filipinos is the most noticeable difference I find in myself. In America, nothing is new, there isn't an interaction that I haven't experienced a dozen times in life, but in the Philippines, I'm on guard. At any time, a situation can present itself that I've never handled before.

There wasn't a lot of interaction to be had that night on the streets, however. For Manila, I thought it was strangely deserted. This was fine with me, I didn't feel like being hounded by a beggar or little girl selling gum already. There'd be plenty of that in Angeles City, which was my destination after the short stopover. I made my way down the thin streets and over a pedestrian bridge across EDSA. Reaching EDSA, I was suddenly not alone, as EDSA is never empty. The wailing of engines and smell of exhaust disturbed my eyes and street vendors hawking everything from sticks of gum to fried chicken made their appearance.

EDSA Complex is a collection of 7 bars (all owned by the same owner) with one of the finest assortments of beautiful girls in the Philippines. Each bar can have as many as 100 young girls working throughout the night. With the scarcity of clientele on that night and most nights I've visited, I often wonder how so many girls can be supported there. I assume that most men are like me, there to find a girl and not to stick around getting loaded as American strip club clientele are apt to do (having a total paycheck slowly teased away), and therefore the total number of male patrons during the night is hard to estimate.

Upon entering the complex, there is a central area with a fountain, restaurant, and entrances to each of the 7 bars. The bars have names like Firehouse Bar and Samba,

6

but I rarely pay attention to the specific bar that I'm in. In my years visiting, I've found they all have similar prices and the quality of girls will rotate amongst them, so believing Firehouse is the better one is a matter of personal experience, though that seems to be where I always end up first, maybe because it is counter-clockwise when entering.

Firehouse Bar is arranged with a long stage on the right wall with a bar running the length of it. Since there were no customers in the bar when I arrived, the girls were all sitting in their assigned spots on the stage and a waitress at the bar stood up and clapped twice to indicate they should proceed to dance after I made my entrance. Being my first night, that was awkward.

Trying to shake off my bashfulness, I walked straight to the stage and took a seat, without even strolling down the bar checking out the now standing girls. There were ten girls laid out down the stage solely for my viewing pleasure. They were all beautiful, wearing a skimpy black bikini with tasteful hair and makeup. None of them had bad teeth or stretch marks, they were the attractive group that gets picked up early.

The waitress, older but also attractive wearing a white tied shirt and black skirt, followed to my seat and took my order for one San Mig Lite[1]. By this time, the three girls on stage in front of me had begun dancing seductively. When I noticed this, I smiled like a king. These girls were showing themselves off to me in hopes I would choose to mate with them. Ok, maybe they were more interested in the money than the mating, but I didn't concern myself with that.

The girl directly in front of me looked 18. She was shorter than the others with a broad frame and nice mounds for breasts. Her face was flat, with a small nose, and wide mouth. Her smile was cute, but she seemed shy,

---

[1] Short for San Miguel, and Philippine bear and quite tasty for the price.

even though she was making eye contact and motioning toward me with her hips like the two girls beside her. Unlike them, I sensed she wasn't entirely comfortable with where she was. I began some facial flirts back to her, and she responded with smiles and a gesture she'd like to sit with me.

As the waitress arrived with my San Mig Lite, she asked, "You want buy girl a drink? Choose."

Ah, this is what I flew 8,000 miles for, to be hounded for drinks after sitting for less than a minute. It's part of the process, and I was used to it, though I was not quite settled in yet and answered her like a rank amateur, "Sure, I'll buy her a drink," pointing to the 18-year-old in front of me. *Give me a break, I was just off the plane!*

The girl on stage bent down to grab her long fishnet jacket to cover herself as she exited the stage. Once her gaze turned away from me, her face went cold, like she was now going through the motions of work and not thrilled to be doing it. It's a reaction that may seem normal to inexperienced go-go bar patrons but I knew I could find a girl who was genuinely happy about being picked, it would just take time.

I would go ahead and buy a drink, I decided. I thought it would lessen the attention on me being the sole customer in the bar. I could relax, have a conversation, and look around.

"Hello, what's your name?" the 18-year-old asked as she arrived at my barstool.

"I'm Nate, what's yours?"

"Nat?" she asked.

"Yes," I answered not caring to go through the correction process.

"Hi Nat, I'm Rosy."

"Let's sit at a table," I said standing up and motioning to the back. I no longer wanted to sit on the stage as my field of vision was now limited to just two girls. We moved to a high table that afforded a full view of the bar.

After Rosy and I arrived at the back table, she sat expressionless peering toward the stage waiting on her drink. I didn't bother trying to make conversation and instead watched with her the happenings in the bar.

A group of Asian customers entered the bar and sat at a larger table in front of us and received immediate attention from waitresses and some girls who were sitting around. The girls on stage tried to draw their attention as well, and I felt better no longer being the lone customer in the bar.

"How long have you worked here? I asked Rosy.

"Two months," was the answer. I didn't think she was even that much past her 18th birthday.

I was preparing to launch a series of questions to determine her age and how she came to work in the bar, when a truly stunning girl walked up to the table. She had long highlighted hair, the face of Charmane Star[2] and the body of a young Britney Spears. I was speechless and my jaw dropped. She didn't make eye contact, but delicately grabbed a napkin from the table and walked away slowly. As I lusted after her gorgeous backside, I concluded she was attempting to get my attention, since there were plenty of other tables from which to grab a napkin, but didn't directly engage me out of respect to Rosy.

Rosy was now irrelevant to me, and she finished her drink with both of us remaining mostly silent. Once finished, she knew there would be no further drink and said, "Thank you sir" and went on her way. I looked around until I caught the gaze of Ms Charmane sitting at a table in the back. I smiled at her and nodded my head, to which she returned the smile and trotted over exuding confidence.

"Hello, what's your name?" she asked, and we

---

[2] Charmane Star – Philippine porn star from late 90s & 00s.

proceeded through the standard questions, until she asked, "Where are you staying?"

It's a strange question to get so early from a bargirl as they usually don't care. Any place is better than the shack they likely live in. I realized by her reaction after my answer that she was picking her customers carefully. She was looking for a rich sugar-daddy or a business traveler she could pick the pocket of, not an experienced sex tourist staying in a pay by the hour hotel. Why she was even interested in the first place with my ratty jeans and plain white tee shirt, I have no idea.

What started out wonderful, with the personality of a truly fun sex worker to go with a supermodel body turned into the same personality I received from Rosy. Could I have still barfined[3] her and taken her to the Victoria Court and fucked the hell out of her? Yes. Would it be what I was looking for? No, it would likely be filled with attitude and be only slightly more enjoyable than jerking off while she sat naked beside me. After one drink, she went on her way as well.

Don't be afraid to case a go-go bar before sitting down and buying drinks.

As I sat there nursing my 2nd beer, I was determined to put the Firehouse Bar behind me and remembering my usual strategy in EDSA Complex vowed not to make the same mistake in the following bars by planting myself in a seat. Don't be afraid to case a go-go bar before sitting down and buying drinks.

I moseyed out the door and into the central area which had turned into a lively place since I arrived now almost an hour earlier. Some girls still in their bar uniforms stood around near the restaurant and door girls

---

[3] Barfine – A fee paid to the bar to take the girl out. Unless notified, it is assumed to include sex.

had positioned themselves in front of the other bars. I went into the next bar on the right.

My entrance was more unnoticed than the Firehouse Bar, which is the way I liked it. I strode around in front of the side stage catching the eyes of some less than attractive dancers searching for that single drink to make their night worth it. I'd pass. The few attractive girls I saw in this bar seemed busy with the Asian clientele. On to the next bar.

The next bar was bigger and my entry made an impression on the multitudes of waitresses and dancers looking to make a buck. I was immediately accosted by two waitresses motioning me to a seat. I walked with them so as not to be rude, arrived at the table in front of the stage, and stood there looking around ignoring their requests for my drink. I hovered over the table for at least 10 minutes not finding any girl that I wanted to buy a drink for, until one waitress, the uglier of the two, became impatient and began demanding I buy a drink.

"Hey, you have to buy drink!" she scolded.

Well, I was convinced… and made my way out of the bar, much to her displeasure.

I was borderline discouraged, guessing that I'd soon settle on a girl just to have the deed done and get some sleep. Though I put importance on the first girl of the trip, there would be plenty of time to find the right girls. I entered the 4th bar and slowly rounded the large stage not eyeing any attractive dancers, and then I saw the first girl since Firehouse I wanted to talk to.

She was leaning against a high stool next to a small back bar wearing a white bikini with a long white netted jacket that draped off the sides of her arms exposing the front of her body to the bar. She had thick straight black shoulder-length hair that must have been a real pain to brush. Her wide Filipino smile with plush full lips sported bright red lipstick and her makeup was tastefully appointed with pink blush and light black eye liner. She had a voluptuous sexy body, with breasts slightly large in proportion to her hips and a body that carried a layer of thick skin which at her age, I'd guess 19, made her look mature and sensual, but that at an older age might suggest a weight problem. The fair skin on her entire body was blemish free and carried no trace of tan.

She was deep in conversation with two other girls who were lounging around the bar and her first reaction when I approached was not one of excitement. It was more of an "oh, I guess I have a job to do now" reaction. She turned to me, smiled, and gave me the standard "hello sir."

"What's your name?" I asked her.

"Nicole... and you?" she replied.

"I'm Nathan."

"Hi Nathan," she said on the first try. I'd guess she had met another Nathan in her line of work.

Though I tried to move in on my newfound beauty and hint to the other girls that I was not interested, one of her friends would not budge and began to hang on me. Being right off the plane, I was in no state to shew away an attractive young girl showing a desire for me. I simply wrapped my arm around her as Nicole continued her relaxed lean on the bar stool.

"You are so handsome, where are you from?" asked the skinny mature looking girl hanging on me whose hands were now finding their way to my crotch.

It's hard to believe that being called handsome would ever get old, even though I didn't really believe it. After a week or so in the Philippines, the statement wouldn't mean much more than "hi" to me, but at that moment, it made my pride stand up and my desires kick in. Here was a sexy young girl, who I would have had no shot with just 24 hours ago, letting me know that I could have her in my bed all night. All I would have to do is say the word, and fork over a bit of cash, of course.

12

Even more astonishing is the fact that this girl did not interest me in the slightest. I was honed into the barely-legal beauty in front of me, knowing that with her as well, I needed only to say the word. Again, just 24 hours ago back in America, as close as I'd get to these girls is if they happened to walk by my coffee shop where they would be unknowingly tickling the libido of an older man longing for his youth. Here, I didn't need youth, I only needed money, and while I knew it was all about the money, it didn't feel that way. These girls were making me feel desired as if I was a handsome young stud at a high school after-party.

"I'm from Las Vegas," I answer Las Vegas in the Philippines instead of America as due to the popularity of Manny Pacquio, they've all heard of it.

"Ooooh, very beautiful!" answered the skinny one.

A waitress appeared and took an order for three drinks, and I decided to sit down and nudge the aggressive girl to slide off. I liked her flirtations, but I was still locked into the beauty that brought me there.

"So, how long have you worked here?" I asked her.

"About five months," she answered turning to me. I began engaging her in a way that they both became aware of who I was interested in.

Five months was an answer that told me she was experienced. I even assume the answer to this question is on the low side of the truth. She was not right off the bus, which would explain her laid back demeanor.

While we finished our round of drinks, the flirting continued from the skinny one while Nicole continued her relaxed lean on the stool and smiled. I became enamored with her full lips, imagining how soft they would be against my lips and on a certain appendage. When the waitress showed up to ask if I'd buy another drink, I had planned my question.

"So, do you like kissing?" I asked Nicole. "I'll buy

another drink if you give me a kiss."

Nicole laughed.

"I like kissing, but I just put on my lipstick!" she exclaimed.

"Oh, I don't mind," I pleaded.

"No, no," she said, shaking her head.

I was disheartened momentarily. She said she liked kissing but the fact that she wouldn't kiss me made me wonder if she'd be shy in bed. It would ruin the night if I could not lock with those beautiful full lips while inside her.

The skinny one didn't waste time, grabbed my face and laid a massive smooch on me. She was working me, but I still wasn't interested. I was taking Nicole to the Victoria Court with me or I was going to the next bar.

"Wow! She really likes you!" said Nicole giggling.

"What about you? You don't like me?" I asked her.

Nicole smiled and said, "You're handsome! Of course, I do!"

That was all I needed to hear. I shook my head to the waitress declining a second drink, and then said to Nicole, "Can I barfine you?"

"Really?" she acted genuinely surprised, and I wondered if she was truly unaware that I made a beeline across the bar to her.

"If you want to," I replied.

"Yes! Of course!" Nicole exclaimed. She came alive in excitement, and I knew I had made a correct decision, if lucky in some way since she seemed to show no interest in being barfined beforehand.

The mama-san eventually showed up, an older Filipino lady that at one time was probably an attractive bargirl herself. She asked for the 1,900 peso barfine and another 3,000 for Nicole. It seemed they had a new procedure in asking for both portions in the bar, and there was some bad news as I had not expected to need 5,000 pesos for the barfine and the drinks would put me over the amount I had. I explained that I had more money in the hotel.

"If it's ok with her, you can pay her the 3,000 pesos later, but I will still need the 1,900 now," the mama-san answered. *Done.*

Once it was all settled, Nicole notified me she'd be right back, and I leaned against the stool she'd been leaning on all night and let the butterflies fester in my belly. Nicole was beautiful, though I'd been through the process of buying a beautiful girl's company many times, it always feels surreal on the first night. The anticipation built until she finally appeared from the back wearing a one-piece tight blue shoulderless dress with black high-heels. She had removed her bright red lipstick and toned down her eye shadow and blush. To me, she appeared even more stunning.

As she approached, a bright smile showing perfect white teeth appeared on her face which beamed with happiness. She walked straight up to me, grabbed my shoulders and pulled herself in and up to lock her lips with mine. The kiss was passionate and real, as if she had a crush on me, and my body returned the fire. I wrapped my arms around her waist, gently caressing the top of her solid young butt and lost track of the world, I didn't care to be any other place. She was everything I'd been waiting on the past several months.

I knew from the moment she laid that kiss on me that this would be one of the best fuck sessions I'd ever had. A sex worker can be good in bed and they can fake being into you, but Nicole was not faking it, whatever the reason, she was into me, she was going to enjoy our encounter.

I leaned against that stool for several minutes making out with her and blocking out the giggles in the bar. When I finally pushed her away, she again beamed a brilliant smile with a look of joy on her face. I smiled back and said, "Are you ready to go?" to which she nodded, grabbed my hand locking fingers, and walked with me out of EDSA Complex.

Entering the first cab, the driver said, "It'll be 200 pesos ok?"

This was a drastic overcharge for a ride that should have been 50 pesos, though this is the standard practice at EDSA Complex, it's very hard to get them to use the meter.

"200?" Nicole asked incredulous, and spoke to him in Tagalog. Nicole was surprising me at every turn. Even after spending significant time with a girl in the Philippines, it is unusual to find one willing to back me up on matters concerning other Filipinos.

"I'll give you 100, final offer, I think she's willing to walk," I interrupted. I didn't need her help, and doubted she'd get anywhere. The driver nodded and we were headed toward the Victoria Court.

"100 is bullshit," said Nicole as we pulled away.

"Don't they usually charge more outside EDSA?" I asked her, knowing it was a foreigner price.

"Yes, it's bullshit."

Taxis in the Philippines have meters and usually they are willing to use them. Occasionally drivers, like in all countries, will try to take advantage of foreigners, and especially outside sex shops. I don't mind too much, which is probably part of the problem. 100 pesos is so much less than any taxi in America, it feels as though I'm robbing them.

Less than five minutes later, I was opening the door to my room at the Victoria Court and found myself alone with the beautiful Nicole who walked into the room and began to look around. It didn't seem like she'd been there before.

She checked the bathroom, and then walked to the window and peered out for a moment. During this time, I sat on the bed and relaxed and waited for her to initiate anything. When she finished her investigation of the room and sat on the opposite end of the bed with the towel and pink condom between us, she did something I'd never seen before and didn't register as odd at the time. For a sex worker though, it was damn peculiar.

She picked up the pink condom, giggled, and flung it to the floor at the end of the bed.

"I'm going to shower," she stated and headed toward the bathroom with her purse.

"Ok, I'll come with you," I said.

"Oh No! I'm shy!" she said smiling.

"You weren't shy at the bar with everyone watching," I reasoned.

"I was just so glad you picked me, you are so handsome!" she said.

At this ego swelling exchange, I could no longer help myself, I chased her toward the bathroom, grabbed her and locked my lips with hers. She reciprocated, but held the door frame to not allow me into the bathroom with her. After a short kiss, I relented and said, "Ok, hurry and take a shower. Do you want me to take a shower too? I just showered before I went to the bar."

"It's ok, it's up to you," she said and closed the bathroom door behind her.

Many things were going to be "up to me" very shortly.

I removed my clothes and laid down on the bed and caught another sight of that middle-aged unattractive man I'd seen earlier hanging out on the ceiling, this time he was naked. There was something different about him though,

17

he was more radiant, more alive. I was happy to know him.

A short time later when Nicole emerged from the bathroom wearing only a white towel, I was still naked on the bed and seeing her ready to service me, I began to grow hard immediately. Nicole smiled, giggled softly and slowly strode toward the end of bed where she put her right hand on her cheek and said, "Sexy man! Are you ready for me?"

"Can't you tell?" I asked referring to my dick which was already verging on full erection.

Nicole stretched her left arm out for balance and with her right hand grabbed the top of the towel and pulled it sideways revealing her youthful voluptuous body. Her breasts were large for her small size and had the firmness of an 18-year-old with small erect nipples. Her whole body was covered with a soft layer of skin, including her flat stomach and wide pelvis with her shaved pubic region and I could just barely make out the small clit slipping out of her closed lip vagina. She was the most beautiful thing I'd seen in months.

She dropped the towel, and her smile grew even wider as she saw the look on my face. She giggled as she slid forward onto the bed and crawled over my naked body letting her nipples caress my balls and then my stomach as she reached in to smother my mouth with another sensual kiss. She lowered her hips gently over my erection and let her body weight sit fully on me, her clean soft skin contacting my whole torso.

I grabbed both cheeks to find her bubbly butt fit perfectly in my hands while she slid her tongue even deeper in my mouth. I was shaking with the release of hormones as this young sex object attacked me passionately.

After a few minutes, she lifted up, smiled and looking into my eyes, repeated, "You're so handsome!"

I leaned forward for another kiss but she had other ideas. She began to slide down my body kissing my nipples and belly until her face reached my hard cock. She gently kissed and grabbed it with her left hand, then lowered her face even more until she was slightly buried by my pubic hair.

I flinched when I felt her tongue press hard against my perineum and then forcefully work up to my balls eventually engulfing them entirely in her mouth. Nicole was enthusiastic and she was loving it. Finding a nympho sex worker doesn't seem like it would be a difficult task but having a young girl attack me in this way on the first night we were together was rare.

Her face looked possessed when she lifted up to position my cock toward her mouth. Then she dropped her head around my dick with such force that I could feel the mattress exuding pressure against my butt. With a quick and deep up and down motion, she wrapped her mouth tightly around my cock so that her tongue and the roof of her mouth were firmly compressed against it.

I leaned my head back to see in the ceiling her gorgeous hair bouncing on my dick with her ass spread open in the air over my feet as she used her curled knees to get leverage. I placed one hand on her head to help her bounce and to admire myself – the dork in the mirror was suddenly a champion sporting a sly smirk, relaxed and casually holding this beauty's head on his dick.

My hand on the back of her head caused her to work furiously for a couple minutes until finally she popped her head off and extending her tongue over her lower lip, gasped for a full breath. She then looked into my eyes and smiled like a cheerleader at a ball game.

I was enthralled and wondering what she would do next, I put my hands behind my head and just returned her gaze. She kissed my dick a little but then began to make the motions of moving herself up my body until she was in a position straddling my hips and I felt the damp lips of her pussy come in contact with the base of my dick. She gave me a few smooches and then lifted her upper body until she was vertical over my crotch.

It was that moment that I realized she did not intend to grab the condom on the floor or ask me to bag up. My eyes opened wide as my brain instantly began to grapple with the confusion of my primal mating urges as a sex starved man with a seductive young trophy versus the fear of contracting a disease from a prostitute or knocking up a young woman. Despite my lengthy experience as a sex tourist, it was an extremely rare occurrence for me, and I did not possess the unconscious competence I'd need to handle it. On one hand, I didn't mind condoms, I was used to them and I wouldn't have given it a second thought if she had presented the option to me. On the other, the dream of entering her naturally was now real, and I suddenly longed for it.

She lifted her right leg so she could prop herself up with her foot while her left leg remained on her knee next to my hip. She now had space between my dick and her pussy and her young thigh spanned out from her tight pussy as it peered toward me. I don't believe she recognized the turmoil in my mind at that moment as she smiled sensually, bit her lower lip, and grabbed my cock propping it up against her near soaked pussy lips. There was not any action I was capable of taking at this moment. The encounter, my emotions, and my dick were entirely in her hands.

She gently thrust her pelvis, with the experience of a professional, to create downward pressure on the head of my dick until it slowly slid inside. I glanced up from the beautiful sight to see her smiling face and tongue outstretched licking her upper lip. She was enjoying it more than me, possibly. When she let gravity lower her pussy down over my dick completely swallowing it, we both closed our eyes and moaned in bliss. The natural feel of her warm and thoroughly wet vagina tightly squeezing my entire shaft caused my mind to drift away from all my feelings of concern. I didn't care anymore, it was exactly what I'd always wanted.

Never retracting her tongue, she dropped down to my face and continued with the passionate kissing she'd performed the whole night, though now she was beginning to bounce on my dick as though she'd been craving dick for months. As it became too much effort to continue the smooch, she dropped her head down beside mine giving me a view in the mirror of the body on top of me working it. Her little bubble butt was smacking with waves against me as her arched back twerked with the effort. I grabbed her ass, letting one finger slide over her exposed asshole with every thrust, as she moaned louder and louder.

After some time, she lifted up vertically exposing her body which had now developed a touch of sweat. That didn't stop her though, she began to thrust herself back and forth so as the tip of my dick was grinding the back of her pussy. She placed her hands on my stomach for more leverage and closed her eyes as she exerted herself. I'm not sure if she remembered there was a customer attached to that dick inside her. She seemed fully self-absorbed.

When girls are fucking in this manner, I can last forever… and it seemed like forever. After 5-10 minutes of furious grinding, she either had a muted orgasm or simply collapsed from the effort onto my chest in a wet sweaty mess, her tits slipping across mine. She opened her eyes and looked at me and sighed.

"Are you ok?" I asked.

"Oh, I'm great," was the only answer I received.

I grabbed her with one arm around her lower back and placed the other hand on the bed, and then sitting up, I spun her to the bed never allowing my dick to exit.

Manhandling her little body in this way was easy, and she let out a "weeeeee" during the spin.

"Strong man!" she said in a fit of laughter as she lay on her back under me.

I felt her feet on my ass as she motioned for me to start pounding and I did not want to disappoint. I started wailing away at her tiny pussy while staring at her grinning face.

Within minutes, I was on the verge of orgasm and I began to determine how I wanted it to happen. I could cum inside her... but I've always dreaded knocking up a girl in the Philippines. I was not the type of man to walk away. Besides, maybe that's what she wanted, maybe she wanted to get pregnant by a foreigner, and she would not be the first Filipina with only that thought on her mind.

I decided that was a bad idea and quickly formed a better idea anyhow. I'd cum on those beautiful tits. I began to think through the process of climbing up and propping one knee to the side of her chest for better aim. It would be glorious and I wondered how she would react, so far, she seemed to be good with everything.

Then, an even better idea crossed my mind. Just how much could I get away with and how much was this girl into? I dropped down for another erotic smooch, as we were both becoming sweaty messes. I grabbed her soaked neck and pulled her face into mine with a passionate force, and then I stopped for a moment and looked into her eyes...

"I want to cum in your mouth," I said as a matter of fact.

In the space of a few seconds, her face turned from passion, to one of puzzlement, and then for a moment, I saw a frown and I thought I had crossed a line. Then, in a motion that sent a wave of butterflies from my belly down to my groin, she reached forward and laid another kiss on me.

"Whatever you want, dear," she said, though not looking particularly pleased.

I dropped my body down to her, and began sliding my cock in and out while staring at the full lips on the mouth I planned to aim my cum into shortly. As I rocked back and forth bringing myself to orgasm, I started grinning at her, to which she returned a smile.

"Come on baby, I want you come in my mouth," she said. She seemed to be growing a little excited at the prospect.

"Mmm, yes, I want your cum, come on baby," she continued, having not said much during the whole session, she now came alive.

I was getting closer and I raised up on my arms to ready myself for the leap forward. In response, she dropped her elbows down beneath her to prop her head up ready to catch what was coming.

"Cum in my mouth baby!" she moaned while staring intently at my dick gliding in and out of her.

And in that moment, my orgasm imminent, I leapt forward, letting one knee land beside her and my other leg holding my dick at the perfect height to enter her mouth. I caught myself with one arm on the back wall and with the other grabbed her head to help hold her on my dick. She took me in her mouth without hesitation and I felt my cum drain into the back of her throat in several spurts.

After finishing, I balanced myself to look at her sitting as still as a mannequin, waiting for me to finish with her eyes closed. I did not sense that she had swallowed and I was curious as to what she'd do.

When she realized I was finished and was watching her, she opened her mouth and let my cum drain out onto her chest as she pulled away from my dick. She then turned her head to the side and violently spit out what was left onto the bed.

I held back a laugh and relaxed on the bed beside her.

After a few spits, she looked at me, wiped her mouth, and said, "Blaayackkk!"

I chuckled.

She smiled and raised her hand as if to slap me, "See how you are![4]"

Nicole quickly removed herself to the bathroom to wash out her mouth, and I relaxed onto the bed lost to satisfaction. However, my feelings of contentment were replaced by feelings of worry of just having had unprotected sex with a bargirl, one that I had deemed as experienced even. While it wasn't the first time bareback with a bargirl, it was by far the fastest time between the first monetary transaction and unprotected sex.

How did this happen? She didn't even consider the condom, in fact, she seemed to regard the condom as a joke. She obviously never wore condoms with her customers, and she was beautiful! It's not as if she was likely to have a shortage of barfines. I can only imagine that her first customers spun her some kind of bullshit about condoms so they would not have to use them on the obviously new girl, and none of her girlfriends at the bar had since educated her.

When she came out of the bathroom, she had replaced her dress.

"So, you want to sleep?" she asked, intending to leave.

I did, I was exhausted, and normally I'd be happy with the immediate exit, but I now hoped to gather some knowledge about her sexual experience.

"So, do you ever use condoms?" I came right out with it seeing my time as limited.

"Sometimes, why?" she answered casually.

"Well..." I was going to bumble this conversation up for sure. "You, uh, should really wear them with

---

[4] See how you are – A Filipino expression used in response to a joke made at someone's expense. May also be used in response to a rude or inconsiderate statement or act.

24

customers."

"Why?"

I stared at her blankly. I quickly thought of what I should say at this point, knowing she may have had no education whatsoever into diseases and perhaps even pregnancy. Then I looked at myself as hypocritical to having this conversation with a girl I'd just chosen not to wear a condom with. It's possibly more my fault than hers.

"Do you want a baby?" I asked her.

"No!" she laughed. "I'm on the pill!"

I decided at that to let it go. She did have some knowledge of the consequences of unprotected sex. Whether I would have believed her beforehand if she had wanted me to cum inside her, I'm not sure, but it did satisfy me that she had made her choices, and I felt no need to try to save a prostitute, whom I had just met, from possibly contracting a disease sometime in the future, if she hadn't already.

"Hey, do you have Facebook?" I asked, deciding I wanted to stay in touch with her. At least if I started pissing fire, I could tell her to get some antibiotics. Ok, that's not really the reason. The true reason is she was amazing in bed and I wanted the option of finding her on my way out through Manila!

She connected with me on Facebook, and I let her leave. In the few minutes I had before passing out, I dreamed of being inside Nicole again. Maybe next time, I wouldn't pull out since she gave me all excuse I needed...

CHAPTER 2

Jet Lag and the 16-year-old Don Juan

Strange things happen to your body, energy, and mood when traveling to a faraway time zone over a 24-hour period. On this trip, I took a 4 leg United flight from Las Vegas that departed in the morning and arrived in Manila in the evening. The flight took 24 hours so I arrived in Manila at about 6am US Pacific Time exactly a day after I left. I should be dead tired, right? Well, I absolutely was, but there is no fooling the body, it knows when I'm supposed to sleep.

After the best sex so far in my life with a bargirl, I passed out quickly around 2am Manila time only to wake up at 6am. I tossed and turned a few times, but I knew that feeling, and I might as well get up and get on the way to Angeles City. First for breakfast: Corned Beef, Scrambled Eggs, and Rice. Say what you want about Philippines food, they sure can do breakfast. Even this cheap free meal at the sex hotel in Pasay delivered the tasteful abundance of calories I needed. Finally, I strapped my backpack on and headed down EDSA to catch a bus to Angeles City.

"Where you go, sir?" I jumped at the sudden appearance of a young kid on a bicycle with side car. I guess I still hadn't adjusted to life in the Philippines yet since being heckled and bothered for money is part of any day for a sex tourist in the Philippines and should not have startled me. Pedi-cabs, as they are known, are common in the Philippines especially in places like Pasay where there is a need for short trips. The kid was about 16 years old and seemed like quite the handsome young man. I judged he should be out chasing girls instead of working.

26

"Victory Liner," I told him. I had intended to walk but the kid struck me as someone that deserved a customer. "How much?"

"Only 50 pesos sir!"

I could not stop myself from chuckling. I remember on my first trip feeling extorted for services such as tour guide or private car. By this trip, I knew most of the going rates and if I wanted to pay 10 pesos I could, but I would pay 20 I decided on the spot. I knew he'd be happy with that and I wouldn't feel like I overpaid. Should I lowball him and meet at 20 or just say 20 and stick to it? Which strategy I decide usually depends on my first impression of the other negotiator. The real hustlers will respect getting lowballed.

While I've learned on vacations to 3rd-world countries not to accept the first rate quoted, to this day I continue to feel uneasy in all matters concerning prices. I cannot explain the way I feel better than Garland, "I get confused with feeling that I shouldn't haggle with poverty, and hating getting ripped off."[5]

What seemed like an eternity later, I was riding towards Victory Liner in a cramped Pedi-cab side car that I had masterfully negotiated down to 40 pesos! Not only did I overpay but I spent so much time getting that extra 10 pesos that I could have practically walked there. This kid was going to make a fortune in his life if he could manage to do something besides pedal around tourists.

"How old are you kid?" I asked after I finished ridiculing myself.

"16 sir!" ... nailed it.

"Where you go sir? Angeles City?" he asked.

"Is it that obvious?" well yes, it was. We foreigners like to think that we look like plain tourists but the truth is they all know the ones of us there for the women.

"Every American go to Angeles City, sir!" he said

---

[5] The Beach, page 51, by Alex Garland

giggling. "You want sex, right?"

"Don't we all kid?" I asked, amused at his candor. "What about you, you popped a girl's cherry yet?"

"Yes sir, many times, I'm master!" he answered, and I believed him. Filipinos seem to know how to get laid and this kid being so handsome probably already knocked up a few girls by now. I hope he doesn't get stuck on a Pedi-Cab for his whole life.

"What? You mean your girlfriend?" I asked fishing for him to continue.

"Ah, ha ha ha," he laughed. "I don't want girlfriend! I just want boom boom many girls!"

'Boom Boom!' This is likely the first time I had heard a Filipino man, or almost a man, say 'Boom Boom.' It is quite a common saying in Thailand, but in the Philippines, I've only heard it in the bars of Angeles City. This kid must have heard it from another sex tourist.

"'Boom Boom?' where did you hear that?" I asked laughing hysterically.

"I Boom Boom all day! Everyone wants to Boom Boom you know?"

Never being able to extract from him where he heard the phrase 'Boom Boom' I let it go. To this day it remains a mystery. But he's right, everyone wants to Boom Boom!

The Victory Liner bus route to Angeles City seems to be the best deal you'll ever find for transportation in the Philippines. Their buses are clean and air conditioned and they don't hold the buses forever attempting to fill them. When searching for the bus to Angeles City, it is Dau that is the proper destination, but don't worry, just look lost in the bus terminal as a foreigner and someone will point you to the bus to Dau.

Stepping off the bus in Dau is a different experience from Manila. At least the area around Pasay and EDSA, though it may be dirty and smelly, you really don't get a sense of the poverty in the Philippines. That changes instantly in Dau and around Angeles City as shacks and beggars are commonplace. On my first trip, though I'd traveled to some 3rd world countries such as Mexico, I was taken aback at how often I would be asked for money and followed around being pestered. Since then, I've taken the position of never offering money to beggars on the street.

It's not that I'm heartless, it's simply that it causes too much trouble. If I give one beggar a few coins, I will be accosted by any beggar who happens to see it and maybe even a few opportunistic passersby who decide to briefly take up the profession. My friend, Jim, who I'll meet with shortly, even goes so far as to say the beggars are part of a syndicate and most of the money they earn from begging will go to someone other than who you are giving the money to on the street. I'm not sure I buy the sinister conspiracy he places on it, and would assume if the money went anywhere besides the beggars themselves, it would be to a family member.

That said, I do believe in a bit of charity while I'm visiting the Philippines. It is a way to assuage the guilt I feel at passing by all the poverty on the street on my way to indulge in a paid relationship with a beautiful young lady who would have nothing to do with me if only she had been born elsewhere. I pick my charity very carefully however, often looking to help out someone who is hard working or a family who is living on the street but not looking to get by simply by begging. I've met visitors who go so far as to look for young men and women who are seeking an education but can't quite afford it. In any event, whether you partake in charity during your visits or not, do it in a way that will give you the greatest satisfaction and don't feel brow beat into it the first time you step off the bus.

"100 pesos to Pacific Breeze?" I ask the first trike driver I see.

"Yes?" he asks. I hate it when they do that: say 'yes' but in a questioning tone[6]. I got in the trike and double checked he understood Pacific Breeze.

Pacific Breeze is my go-to hotel for trips to Angeles City. It used to be one of the nicest available but in its age has been relegated to a standard good value in Angeles City. The location is perfect, the rooms are clean, large and quiet, and there is a decent restaurant always staffed with friendly and charming young girls. And that is where I went first to get some coffee and French fries and hope the lingering sleepiness would abate.

"Hey, where's Sai?" I asked to the bubbly young waitress behind the bar in the restaurant. Sai was a waitress there that I had developed a bit of a rapport with over the past couple trips and I was as eager to see her again as anyone in town, even though there was nothing more between us than a friendly customer-waitress acquaintance.

"Sai? Who is Sai?" she asked and turned to another girl to speak Tagalog. I was a little heartbroken at that point as Sai was the senior waitress on day shift so it was obvious she no longer worked there.

"Sai quit, she's taking care of her family," answered the other girl.

"Oh man, she doesn't work anywhere? She didn't change to Central Park?" I asked with little hope. The same company that owns Pacific Breeze had recently opened a new tower hotel called Central Park. Many of the girls left Pacific Breeze earlier but Sai had stayed as she felt more comfortable.

"No no, she is only mother now."

---

[6] Filipinos will often agree with you if they don't understand. When it's important, such as transportation, it pays to double check.

"I'll take a coffee and some French Fries please."

"Ok sir. Brewed coffee yes sir?" answered the bubbly waitress, really more of a statement than a question. She knew Americans didn't drink instant coffee[7].

After a great first night and a fun transfer day, I had my first disappointment. As with any vacation but especially vacations when traveling by myself, I enjoy seeing people that I met on previous trips. I liked Sai. I knew she was off-limits and had a family but that didn't change my desire to see her and spend my afternoons before bar hopping flirting with her in the Pacific Breeze restaurant. Now, I wasn't even so sure I wanted to stay at Pacific Breeze.

Even though I gorged myself on coffee, I had to fall asleep that late afternoon but as is typical with the jet lag battle, I was wide awake two hours later. That was almost perfect, I reasoned, I'd have plenty of energy for a bar hop!

I phoned my friend Jim who was expecting me. Jim is a fellow American who retired to Angeles City at the young age of 40 and had lived there for a little over 10 years. We get along because in most ways we are just alike. We are both very average looking, not tall, receding hairlines, not skinny but not too fat. We are capable of getting tans but usually prefer the computer to the outdoors, we both love paying for sex, don't really enjoy the company of women beyond sex but are respectful of women nevertheless, and neither of us are sloppy drunks. That last qualification is not always easy to find in a friend in Angeles City.

---

[7] Filipinos drink instant coffee, usually the NesCafe brand. It is bearable but only with sugar and cream. If you are a black coffee drinker, don't even bother with it, find a place that caters to foreigners.

As for being respectful of women: I've spoken to people, usually state-side, that would deem the mere act of paying for sex as disrespectful. Opinions vary widely on the subject. For the men who visit Angeles City, their levels of respect for the women they buy sex from vary widely. I've met men who go not really for sex, but for the opportunity to treat a woman as if she was a slave, and in some cases men go there looking for the innocent girl off the bus from the province so they can degrade her in ways that might land them in jail any place else. I can only assume what causes this type of attitude, whether it is something they were born with or they are holding some sort of grudge from their earlier life experiences. There are many of these kinds of sex tourists, thankfully most simply push boundaries in bed.

On the other end of the curve, and fortunately more numerous, are guys like Jim and myself. We are simply boring men who are not all that charming and capable of picking up women. For myself, I'm plain fearful of engaging in the song and dance that constitutes courting a woman. We may not be good with women but we hold no animosity towards them for it. The problem lies in the fact that our sex drive is alive and well. We simply want a relationship with a woman that includes sex, and we want that relationship to be as mutually beneficial as possible, whether it be because we are paying for it or any other reason. The men in this group tend to have various opinions as to how much of a relationship they want. Some men visit Angeles City for sex but deep down actually desire a wife – and they usually have no problem finding one.

After my light lunch and nap, I was plenty hungry again and agreed to meet Jim at a restaurant near his house instead of asking him to drive down to the Pacific Breeze. Yes, he has a car. It's an old beater that he paid almost nothing for, but is better than a scooter which I see many foreigners riding. Being from the desert, I just can't handle scooters. The idea of getting wet when trying to get somewhere is about as scary to me as driving on the streets in the Philippines. It does rain a ton in the Philippines. It is sudden and brutal when it happens, not a refreshing shower like we get in the American Southwest.

"Hey Nate, long time man, what's it been a whole 6 months?" Jim asked sporting a welcoming smile. We both knew what he meant by that. For having an entire ocean to get across, I just couldn't stay away and had to get back to the male fantasy land.

We took a seat at Bretto's, a deli that he had picked out up the road a bit from the bar district. I was pleased with the selection of cold sandwiches, a type of food seriously lacking in the Philippines. This is the great thing about finding local friends to hang out with, they usually have far better knowledge of the local restaurant scene. Near Fields Avenue, the restaurants are either overpriced or not good. I would lump the restaurant at Pacific Breeze into the overpriced category though the food is just fine.

"Still not married? What's wrong with you? You are always alone when you meet me!" I said, razzing him a little. Though it's true, in the two years we've been hanging out, he's never once had a girlfriend of any kind, which I highly respected. Why bother?

"Oh, I just can't do it. I see some of the expats here get completely screwed by some of these girls," he said with something obviously on his mind. "A friend I made when I moved here is fighting with his girlfriend over the house he built for her."

"It wasn't in his name?" I asked, still in the American mindset.

"Well sort of, but you can't really put a house in your name as a foreigner. There are some lease deals and mumbo jumbo that can be done, but at the end of the day the house is in HER name and us foreigners don't have the rights we'd expect.

"Come to find out, he's a friggin' idiot though. She moved in so-called 'family' to the house for cooking and cleaning and driving and such. Turns out the driver was her Filipino boyfriend, so the situation is very awkward. I suppose it's just a typical career bargirl that snagged the biggest fish to move to town."

I've heard stories like that before. It's the kind of story that gets told a lot. A rich older Westerner moves to the Philippines and falls for a hot 20-year-old beauty who is only interested in the money he has and proceeds to milk him for as much as she can, even getting houses built for her and her family. There is the alternate story path with girls marrying Westerners and moving to America, Europe, or Australia and promptly divorcing after 2 years having only been seeking a way out of the country.

These are mostly fear tactics told by the men who frequent places like Angeles City. While you may be asking for trouble looking for love in a bar, a majority of the relationships I hear of having formed there turn out to be loving partnerships, even the ones with a huge age disparity, so long as the man never loses sight of that fact. Bring a bargirl to America and spoil her, and she'll likely clean your shit up until the day you die. Bring the same girl to America and ask her to get a job, and she'll quickly look to better her situation either with a rich man who won't make her work or a young man she can have a traditional family with.

"But enough of that, I haven't been bar hopping in a month you know. I probably won't pick out a girl with you, but I would love to hit the scene and have a few beers," Jim said.

"Why on earth would you not get a girl? Have you had your fill? God, I wish I could live here." I said.

"Just do it. Pack up your shit and come on out, just like I did," Jim demanded.

34

I'd heard all that on every trip. How some guys can peel themselves away from their comfortable American life, I just haven't been able to work out. I'm quite happy being the occasional Sex Excursionist.

"I only hope I can pick up a girl myself tonight," I said. "Since I got here last night, I've had a total of maybe five hours of sleep to go with the few I had on the plane."

… Actually, I planned to get two girls that night.

CHAPTER 3

The Door Girl with no ID

She doesn't have an ID? Scary. Well, it doesn't have to be scary, because she should simply be considered off limits. In Angeles City, every girl working in a bar must wear a set of IDs that show her real name, age, health checkup status, and even her virginity status. There are no exceptions to this, even the horridly fat waitresses and girls who won't leave with a customer must have them, and so my skepticism of her claim that door girls didn't need the IDs was fully justified. I knew that I'd be taking more risk than I should if I brought this sweet, charming, beautiful, albeit young looking girl to my hotel.

After we finished dinner, we squeezed into Jim's tiny car and cruised towards Walking Street until he found what he was looking for. There was a middle-aged Filipino standing in front of a row of parking places as if a guard, but not wearing a uniform[8]. Jim waved to him and the man pointed us down to an empty parking space, and then stepped into traffic with his hands in the air and directed us off the road. Jim whipped his car around and pulled in backwards with the ability of a professional valet, he's done that a few times. As we exited the vehicle, the smiling Filipino and my friend exchanged some

---

[8] A freelancer equivalent to the guys who try to wash your windshield in traffic jams.

pleasantries as the payment of 5 pesos was made for the assistance with the prime parking spot and halting of the Fields Avenue thoroughfare, so we could begin our slow pub crawl down the Angeles City scene.

It was a busy Saturday night and the myriad of obstacles to dodge from beggars, to vendors, to aggressive door girls was daunting even for a Philippines veteran and a local. Not certain where we wanted to end up, we simply roamed around flirting with the odd door girl and peering in the curtains for quick glimpses of the talent on stage. Jim seemed disinterested in everything he saw. Unlike the last trip when he seemed like the charming gentlemen all the girls liked, he hardly said a word to the girls. I wondered if his friend's experience had soured his entire libido.

For that matter, I had not seen much I liked either, until I saw HER. It was not uncommon for me to fall for a door girl first.

She was short and wearing flat shoes, the top of her head coming barely to my shoulder and I'm only 5'7" myself. She wore a long black evening dress revealing only her shoulders and arms. Her hair had yellow highlights and her smile was bright and friendly. She had fair skin and the cutest little face, with wide cheeks and a small nose that identified strictly Filipino.

She grabbed on my arm and playfully ushered me into her bar. She could have taken me anywhere, I was enthralled like a teenage boy shocked by the sudden attention of the popular girl on the block. The journey to the seat in the bar was accompanied by the usual "How are you sir?" and "Where you from?" until the destination she had in mind for me was reached and I found myself alone with my friend in the middle of a small standard Angeles City bar. Wait what? She just left... that doesn't usually happen, my sole reason to be in that bar had vanished back through the curtains.

It's not always the case in Angeles City bars that the hottest girls are manning the door, but it was certainly the case in that bar. Including my new love, the other girls outside had far more sex appeal than the dancers inside. I was ready to make a hasty exit, but Jim was tired of walking and eager to put down a San Mig Lite. The bar was typical of Angeles City with a long stage running one wall and booths spanning the opposite wall. It was obviously managed by westerners, easy to determine by the two 50-year-old white guys running around taking care of business. I'm not sure why, but male western papa-sans don't sit well with me. It's probably due to jealousy. I'm not sure what there is to be jealous of though, as pimping a group of uneducated whores in a foreign country sounds more like misery than living a dream.

Our San Migs were enjoyed mostly over conversation of Western Affairs, as the talent in that bar and the typical bar events had long lost their interest to both of us. Within 10-15 minutes, we were off and heading out the door. Upon exiting, I found my girl and captured her under my arm.

"Hey, why did you run away?" I asked.

She blushed and launched into an apology, "I'm sorry, I didn't know you want me to stay! I'm only door girl." Since we had just started our pub crawl, I pulled away from her and continued on.

"She's probably underage or a cherry girl[9]... or both," Jim remarked to me. He wasn't aware at that point that I was quite taken by her, and though the thought had crossed my mind, I didn't appreciate hearing his virtual agreement that I should forget about her and look elsewhere for my companion. As the night went on, I did forget about her a little, but as was the case during many

---

[9] A virgin. Typically will not barfine, or only for a pub crawl, or may be selling her cherry for a high price. May sometimes be used to refer to a bargirl who won't barfine, virgin or not.

nights in red light districts, I just didn't see another girl that I fancied. Even above average talents at Club Atlantis and Dollhouse, where we stopped into during the pub crawl, didn't offer anything I was interested in.

Passing the Lollipop bar, Jim stopped and said, "Hold on, I need to go in here to see someone. I almost never get down here to Walking Street anymore."

Lollipop bar was a slight upgrade from the earlier bars we went into. It had a stage in the middle with booths on either side. I like these kinds of layouts a little more, this way I get to see tits AND ass.

Before we got much past the door, a little spitfire of a bargirl ran over and practically tackled Jim. "Jim! How are you honey?" she asked as if she'd finally been reunited with her long lost love. Jim gave her a big bear hug in a fatherly type of way, and it seemed to me the relationship was more meaningful than a bargirl-customer one.

Jim and she caught up for 10-15 minutes as I scanned the other girls in the bar. Again, none of them caught my eye, but I downed my 3rd San Mig and was starting to get a little second wind, it seemed I would make it through the night without passing out from jet lag.

Finally, Jim let her go and it was just him and I again and he told me the story with her. She had been a cherry girl in the bar when Jim got to know her. She planned on saving her virginity for true love but would barfine for nights of barhopping and fun and one night she left with a young European man.

She ended up back at his hotel room after having too much to drink and a short time later passed out. She woke up the next afternoon to the hotel ringing the room asking when he was going to check out, but he was gone. It was obvious to her they had had sex and there was a small pool of blood in the bed. Afterward, she had called Jim to pick her up and she had stayed with him for a few nights as she tried to come to grips with what had happened.

39

Had she been raped? Drugged? Well, not even she knew that for sure, but with his hasty departure in the early morning while she lay there asleep, it's likely it wasn't entirely consensual, and he would have ended up in prison in the Philippines had she reported it.

As Jim told me this, I couldn't help but feel a sense of Déjà vu. I'd heard similar stories from bargirls before.

Though a little bit of a buzzkill for me to hear the story, I nonetheless felt sorry for her. She seemed to be doing alright now though and was enjoying her newfound life as a non-cherry bargirl.

For about an hour, we hung out at Lollipops, then Jim said he was tired and ready to head back to the car. It was at this point I remembered the cutie who had tugged on my heart earlier.

Butterflies fluttered in my belly as we made our way back towards the Perimeter of the red-light district where his car was parked. I could remember where the bar was and my imagination began to run the different outcomes of another encounter with her outside the club. Would she even still be there? I knew she would remember me due to our conversation as I left, but would she act interested or would she simply try to do her job as a door girl? And was she even available for barfine? It is common for pretty girls unwilling to barfine to be placed on door duty. Or more to the point... if she barfined, would she be willing to have sex? Like Jim's Lollipop girl, there were plenty of young pretty girls more than happy to be barfined for a night of bar hopping, karaoke, and dancing but with no interest in joining a man at his hotel. As we approached the area with her bar, I could see the black dresses of the door girls outside her bar with one tiny hourglass shape among them, she was still there.

Don't tell a sex worker you are taking Viagra, just take it.

I didn't have much time to say goodbye to Jim as her charming little body and radiant smile ushered me into the bar. I was hers and she knew it, but I still needed to find out how much of me she was willing to have.

The question of whether she would have sex was solved quickly. I spent a little time on the issue of her age and how long she'd been working there and why she didn't have ID's but when I found out she had already barfined and had sex, all my questioning was over. Not only had she been barfined several times, but one of her customers had used Viagra and fucked her pussy raw. She would have sex on a barfine and she seemed like she was going to take whatever was given. Well, she did add that she wasn't going to let a man take Viagra again – there is a lesson here: don't tell a sex worker you are taking Viagra, just take it.

The night was late, so I told her I wanted to go directly to the hotel and that I was jet lagged so I might fall asleep early and she'd have to leave. This was partly true, and partly that I planned to call another girl after her, I was running out of time before I expected to hit the jet lag wall. She was fine with that, this barfine was looking better with each passing sentence. I paid and she disappeared to change clothes.

Seeing her walk out of the back in street clothes was a like a dream and again I felt my heart flip. She wore tight skimpy jean shorts with flip flops showing off every inch of her tiny legs. Her yellow tank top matched the highlights in her hair which all matched the fair Asian skin so atypical for Filipinas. And she was smiling as if she was happy and eager for the night out. At worst, she was going

41

to act like she was enjoying the night and at best, she might actually be interested in me a little.

She tucked nicely up under my arm for the walk back to my hotel. I had trouble keeping up with her energy, she was bouncing and laughing and enjoying herself like young girls should. I could feel my heart being tugged on, what man could not fall for this loveable girl?

"Where are you from?" she asked looking up at me with that beaming beautiful smile.

"Didn't you ask me that already?"

She made a slight recoil, but in the cutest of ways and her smile grew even wider. Then she put her hand over her mouth and chuckled in the innocent bashful way only young girls can. "I'm sorry!"

"Ha ha, it's ok. I'm American," I replied.

"Oh really! I love Americans. You are all so nice!" she said, seeming to be even happier with the way her night was going. I've found that to be the case in the Philippines, they tend to believe Americans are the nicest of all the tourists, though I assume that is a preconceived bias… or they say that about every country.

"What about you? Where are you from?" I asked.

"Leyte"

"Where in Leyte?" I asked. I knew a lot about Leyte.

"Nowhere."

"Oh, tell me, I've been there!"

Again, she looked up at me smiling with the most adorable smile revealing her surprise and pleasure at my answer.

"Really?! You've been to Leyte? I'm from Ormoc," she answered.

Ormoc is a very poor town in the heart of Leyte and was ravaged by Typhon Yolanda that came through a few years previously. I had noticed a lot of girls from there. There must have been a very active mama-san network in that area.

42

"Yes, I've been through there. I traveled from Ormoc to Tacloban shortly after the Typhon," I said hoping to impress her.

"You should come back with me!" she said giggling, and squeezing me gently with her arms around my belly. I'm sure she had no idea how much that idea appealed me at that moment.

It was a short trip back to my room at the Pacific Breeze. I enjoyed the walk to the hotel with her more than anything up to that point in Angeles City. The company of an energetic and joyful young girl will make any man enjoy his time. I only wished I could have walked around the city instead, but we were engaging in a business transaction, something I had sort of forgotten.

In the room, she wasted no time jumping in the shower and in the space of an Indy 500 lap, she was out and I was in. As I came out of the shower, I saw her lying on the bed wrapped in a hotel towel which nearly covered her entire body neck to toe. I might have caught one little glimpse of ankle.

"Lights please," she requested, again with that smile.

"Oh, lights are ok," I insisted.

"No No! Lights out, pretty please," she said with a coy raised voice. I'm sure she was used to getting her way, she certainly knew the right way to carry herself when asking a man for something.

Of course, nice guy that I am, I went over and turned out the hotel lights to which I discovered the room nearly pitch black.

"Thank you. He he," she laughed.

I bumbled over toward the bed feeling around for her body, or the towel covering her body. As she felt my hands contact her, she raised her arms to my neck and coerced me on top of her and unfurled the towel. I pressed my body down onto hers and finally felt the soft fair skin I had become so entranced with back at the bar. Despite her tiny

43

body, she had the firmest perfectly shaped breasts that my hands could engulf entirely.

She was ready with the condom, she certainly had that part down. I would have enjoyed more foreplay but I was ready. I had been ready the moment I laid eyes on her and even though I could no longer see her in the dark room, the mere presence of her was enough to excite me.

In the dark and with her small body, I had trouble penetrating her and I was moving my hips around in a ridiculous attempt to locate where I was supposed to go.

"Haha, you are so bad at sex!" she said giggling, and again surprising me at her nonchalant composer. I laughed in response, as I was feeling terrible at it myself.

I finally managed the task of inserting myself inside of her and felt the squeeze her tight young body produced. She pulled my face to hers and inserted her tongue in my mouth and let out the sexiest of moans. This excited me to the point of getting lost in the moment and the next few minutes are a blur of pleasure in my mind.

Afterward, I collapsed and she rolled up under my arm. Despite the dark room, awkward start, and short time, it was truly a great paid-for sexual experience in every way.

As I was thinking of ways to keep her and blow off the other girl, she got up to get her clothes back on, and I was quickly reminded that bargirls don't often forget when you tell them they can leave right after. And with that, she was gone, but not forever…

CHAPTER 4

The Submissive Girl

It was the legs with Ashley. I met her on a previous trip to Angeles City and had kept in touch on Facebook. She was a waitress at a little hole-in-the-wall bar in the heart of Fields Avenue near High Society[10]. The mama-san there was rather pushy and always drunk. In fact, she would have annoyed me into leaving if I had not hooked up with a wingman who was really into a girl at the bar. As Mama was bringing me girl after girl from the lineup, my eyes kept watching my waitress's legs as she moved around. She was wearing a black dress that had sleeves but quite a short skirt. It was as if all we were supposed to see of the waitresses were their legs.

I kept passing on dancer after dancer even though mama would add certain tidbits about each one. "She good, she go all night. She lick your asshole, you like getting ass licked? She new, tight pussy. She give good blowjob, all night." Or something to that effect. Just to annoy her, I started asking her "anal no condom?" and as intended that stopped the human sex train abruptly and the mama-san wondered off to pester a group of loud obnoxious drunks in the back who probably weren't getting girls until later no matter what she offered.

Shortly thereafter, I started flirting with the waitress. She acted shocked and even shy. I don't know why, along with her legs and slender body, she had a pretty face to round out the package, with long black hair and fair skin.

---

[10] High Society – A dance club on Fields Avenue, a fairly new addition to the scene as of this writing.

It very well might be the Mama-san's fault that she didn't get picked more often. If men were allowed to sit un-pestered, I'm certain their eyes would have been drawn to her more often.

She eventually relaxed with me and I got her to hang on my shoulders and make out a little at which point I asked her if she would like to barfine with me. When she smiled and nodded her head, I yelled out, "Mama!" A few times... and a few more times. Until finally she stumbled over and slurred "Oh you want Ashley? She not do anal!"

Ashley's grin immediately dropped to a scared puppy dog look and I assured her it was a joke with Mama and her ass would remain unspoiled.

My first night with Ashley was nothing special. I did find out she was a single mother from Camiguin, a small volcanic island popular with travelers, which is a little unusual for sex workers in Angeles (the Camiguin part). She had some minor stretch marks and the softer breast associated with mothers, but besides that still maintained a sexy slim body with those amazing legs... having them wrapped around me was a joy. They were slim and soft and I could move them in any angle I desired for the most pleasure.

I asked her how she came to be in Angeles working in a bar and she explained that she had been working at an upscale resort in Camiguin taking care of rich customers and making what amounted to $15/day. One day an older man and his girlfriend from Angeles were drinking late in the hotel bar and they got to talking. Well, I suppose if I was stuck somewhere making a pittance and working my ass off when someone told me I could triple it and work half as much by having a bit of sex, I might do it as well.

During our first night and most of the day after, Ashley seemed quite taken by me. The emotion she was showing me was real, she truly didn't want to leave me and truly wanted to see me again. Future husband material she thought of me? Well, that was probably not going to happen, but I could connect with her on Facebook, seeing her again on my next trip would not be out of the question.

And my next trip had arrived. Although she didn't know I was coming, I knew she was getting ready to go home to Camiguin and give up the bar life. If I was going to see her, I only had 2 days to do it. If she was still attracted to me the way she was on my first visit and the way she seemed to express in various messages online, it should be a fun night. I already had one nut too, so I could wrap those legs around me for a rather long session.

I could feel the shock through messenger when I told her I was in Angeles. I had expected her to be at the bar, but she wasn't. She wanted to see me right away, even though she was busy packing. She said she'd be coming within the hour. *Woh, guess she really needs the money.*

She messaged me again as she was pulling up to the Pacific Breeze in a trike. I was outside in front before she got there. When she saw me, she froze in her tracks. The feelings she had for me before were still strong, and for a moment I was wondering if it was a good idea to meet her. I've had experiences with clingy and jealous Filipinas. Oh well, no reason to worry about that now, she had a plane ticket home in 2 days to see her daughter and I doubted I'd come before her child.

After a few seconds, she still didn't move. She just stood there fidgeting. She was wearing a small skin-tight dress made of cheap fabric and a generic design. Her hair was up in a bun and in the night, I could make out that same slender body and long skinny legs that I'd enjoyed previously. I went to her and as I put my arm around her,

47

she leaned her head into my neck, and said, "I've missed you so much." *Sure you have dear.*

The door man must have thought I was her long lost high school boyfriend... at least he might if I wasn't 20 years older and a foreigner holding a girl that looked like an Angeles City bargirl. With a shy slow move, her arms finally made their way around me and then she allowed us to move into the hotel.

Back in the room, I had trouble breaking through her guarded shy mannerisms. I didn't expect the rest of the night to be lacking sexual activity, but it wasn't happening fast enough for me. She seemed to want to lay on the bed and cuddle for a great deal longer than I'm accustomed to. After 10 minutes, we were still fully clothed. *10 minutes? Come on, I'm not your boyfriend.*

Probably because of the experience with the door girl I just had and the real attraction I felt toward her, I couldn't get interested in Ashley in a manner beyond the act of having sex. It's a shame how our attractions work. Quite likely just a few years previously, Ashley would have been every bit the bundle of joy the door girl had been. One child and a run-out by the baby's father followed by a few years of spreading your legs for money changes a girl.

"I need to take a shower, I'm sorry, I didn't wash before I came here," she finally said to me. Well, get to it I was thinking, this is getting a little stale. Though I had my hands all over those legs while we were cuddling, I was ready to get in between them. At least this explained a little better her reluctance to move past lying on the bed and holding each other.

"I'll shower with you ok?" I asked. I should have known the answer to that question. She could barely bring herself to kiss me and I was asking for her to get naked and wash together? *Silly me.*

I laid back in the bed a little dejected and certainly regretting my decision to let the door girl go, but Ashley shimmied into the bathroom and left the door cracked as she started the shower, and I immediately thought of a way to make this night way more enjoyable. I undressed and snuck into the bathroom about a minute after her.

Pacific Breeze has an open shower, no door or curtain and I could approach her from behind completely unnoticed. I reached in gently and closed both arms around her stomach immersing myself in the shower with her.

"Ahh, Nathan! See how you are!" she screamed, half laughing and half crying. She deserved it for leaving the door cracked! *Amateur hour.*

She let out a long sigh as she came to grips with not being able to avoid a naked embrace any longer. She then relaxed and let her weight lean into me and she locked her hands into mine and began circling her hips in a seductive caressing way against my hardening dick. She was lightening up much faster than I expected.

She turned around and locked her lips into mine, being much taller than the door girl, I did not have to bend down. I roused up fully at the feeling of her lips on mine and she moved her hands down and wrapped my dick in a soapy embrace. In response, I pulled her closer and reached my hand down to her ass and let two fingers gently stroke her asshole and the back lips of her pussy. She moaned in pleasure and shoved her tongue deeper into my mouth.

Barely drying ourselves, we collapsed onto the bed and enjoyed a few more minutes of foreplay complete with partial insertion in both holes by my eager fingers. She then pushed me onto my back and kissed down my chest until she got to my dick. With only a few teasing kisses, she engulfed me in her mouth. I enjoyed a highly experienced deep-throat blowjob. Unbeknownst to her, I could have let her go on like that for an hour or more after the day I'd had, but she only had about 10 minutes of

49

stamina in her before sliding up and putting me inside her, after slipping a condom on. Ashley was more mature concerning condom use, it wasn't an option or even something to be discussed, it was just something that had to be done, and I respected her for that.

After a good 30 minutes of sweaty sex, I finally got my second nut for the day. I tried to control it even longer, but she was going at it like a cardio workout, and I was not so unhappy with my decision to see her again. That is what I remembered about her.

When she collapsed beside me, there was something very different than my earlier guest for the night. She had no intention of getting up shortly thereafter, she was satisfied right where she was. Exhausted and jet lagged, I was feeling that way as well. I was quite happy to have the company for the rest of the night.

As I lay there drifting off to sleep, I reran the wonderful night in my head. I found it disheartening that I felt nothing for Ashley, a girl who seemed to be deeply involved with me emotionally. I couldn't keep my thoughts off the charming door girl that I had spent no more than an hour with. It's too bad we have no control over that kind of thing. With Ashley, the sex was better, she was more mature, and she liked me. If making a rational choice of company, picking Ashley would be a no-brainer, yet all I could think about was getting another shot at the door girl.

Don't inform sex workers of your travel plans.

"Why did you come back now? I go home

tomorrow," Ashley asked me the next morning staring into my eyes after I woke. She then slapped me playfully on the chest with both hands and let out a whimper.

The better question would be why I didn't tell her I was coming, but I wouldn't offer that up. In my first few visits to a sex destination, I made the mistake of making promises to girls that I would see them again, even informing them of my travel plans. This gives them a sense of having a relationship or even some sort of ownership, as if I'm their customer and only theirs. The jealousy that arises can complicate what is supposed to be a fun-filled sex trip and nothing more. Don't inform sex workers of your travel plans.

In fact, I quickly tried to figure a way out of this line of conversation. I believe reaching my hand around to her ass, pulling her forward, and kissing her neck and shoulder was the appropriate answer to that question.

The morning foreplay quickly turned to morning sex, and I had nicely avoided the "let's play girlfriend-boyfriend" game that she was initiating. If she wasn't leaving the following day, I probably would have started easing her out the door, but I figured it would be nice to hang out until then. I wanted to stop by the Clark SM-Mall Movie Theatre to watch The Revenant with Lionardo Dicaprio which had just been released, and having a real date instead of just some bargirl I picked up would make it nicer. Plus, I'm sure she would enjoy it and if I could separate from her without hurting her feelings, even better. It's only two days, I had three more weeks still.

In general, I try to avoid situations like that with girls I paid for sex with. They happen astonishingly often in the Philippines. In other sex destinations like Costa Rica, Mexico, and even Thailand somewhat (have not yet truly experienced Cambodia) the girls are more career-oriented. However, it makes the sex better if the girl is a bit interested in me. I enjoy feeling desired. Sure, the desire probably only exists because of my ability to improve her quality of life, but I'll take it. I'm sure it feels the same for the wealthy man in America who picks up younger girls simply because he has a Ferrari.

When the relationship starts to move beyond sex however, I find it less enjoyable, even if I hold a bit of an attraction to them. I know the result of any relationship I form on a sex vacation – I will return home and likely never see them again. It would do neither of us any good to develop strong feelings. Even less so for them, as they have so little control over how long we are together. The idea of seeing a girl for a couple weeks, developing an attraction to them and then having to state to them I'm not interested in anything further is a little overwhelming to me. I'm a softy. Why bother with that when I can have ten or more one-night relationships in the same period?

After some room service, I decided to check out of the Pacific Breeze and check into Central Park hotel. It is owned by the same Filipino company and I expected to see some of the former Pacific Breeze waitresses that I might know. The rooms were $30US more per night but more modern and with better views. Ashley didn't think much of them, but I accused her of doing the bargirl "you are special no matter what" talk, to which she vehemently denied.

"It's only room. It has Air-con. Same thing," she said. "Elevator is slow."

I had not even noticed the elevator, and to me it wasn't slow except when comparing it to no elevator, which was likely her argument. The roof of Central Park was an outdoor restaurant and pool with a nice view over Walking Street and Angeles City. That is what sold it for me. Without Sai in the closed-in Pacific Breeze restaurant, I'd prefer the more upscale Central Park restaurant for my morning coffee and corned beef. It's a shame though, as the tower is about to be dwarfed by an even larger tower next door. One day I may be sitting in the bar at Central Park watching a bargirl taking cock in a hotel room in the adjoining tower.

I found my afternoon session with Ashley to be a little more strained. Whether it was the jet lag or simply from overloading my out-of-practice testicles, I had trouble staying interested or even hard. I didn't give up though and managed another nut after she agreed to blow me for as long as it took. Actually, the obedient offer is what perked me. A subservient beautiful woman bouncing her head up and down on my cock for the whole afternoon was a delightful idea, but unfortunately combining the idea with the action produced an accelerated end to the session from what just a few minutes ago seemed destined to take ages.

Afterwards, I was happy to leave the hotel and walk with Ashley to SM Mall. As I passed the occasional trike I would question "SM 50 pesos?" to which I usually got the reply of "100," as we kept walking. I was fine to walk the short distance but I knew Ashley didn't really want to, *they never do*, even though she had agreed. Attempting to find a ride for the much more reasonable rate of 50 pesos, though still very expensive for the Philippines, was my way of making myself look good if we couldn't find a cheaper ride and a way to live with myself for not forcing her to walk if we could.

As we rounded the corner by Phillies[11], I engaged what I determined to be my last trike driver and though he declined, as we passed he clapped his hands and yelled in Filipino to a relaxing trike driver further down the street who jumped up eagerly, started his trike and swung it swiftly towards us. I said "SM," he acknowledged with a nod and off we went. Less than 60 seconds later we were walking through the doors to SM Clark and I still didn't

---

[11] Phillies – A fun bar with pool tables near the intersection where Walking Street becomes Fields Avenue.

think it was worth 50 pesos.

It was busy on that weekday in SM, though I've never been in a Philippine mall when it didn't seem busy. In an American mall, you'd have to assume there was a special event, like Black Friday, and even then, you'd think it was busy. Although I'm not adept at dealing with any crowds, I'm borderline incompetent with Filipino crowds. Whether it's engrained in the culture or a product of every public place being jammed with people, the habits of Filipinos concerning taking space seems to be "If there is a space to be filled, I must fill it, and if I get there first, I win." Sometimes I feel it's like playing chicken. Of course, I'm always the first to balk. When it comes to lines, you must keep a tight distance between you and the person in front of you. In the Filipino mind, any space where a human being could fit would indicate a break in the line and that space should naturally… be filled.

Fortunately, there was no line to deal with at the theatre, and we relaxed to a rather mediocre Leo movie which I'm sure Ashley truly hated. In spite of that, she resisted all my attempts at theatre naughtiness, beyond simple cuddling. I guess it's the fault of the old Filipino lady that chose our row out of a mostly empty theatre. It's ok, I'd had two nuts so far and they were unlikely to be the last nuts of the day so I begrudgingly relaxed and feigned enjoyment of cuddling.

After the movie, we walked through various stores pretending to be a loving couple while I waited to be asked for a present. That request never came in the slightest, not even a gesture to something that she liked or wanted. Again, my respect for Ashley built, but not my desire for her. In fact, with each passing hour, it seemed I was becoming exponentially more exhausted of her company. If I was in an American mall taking this girl through stores, every man would think I'd done quite well for myself. Here in Angeles City, she was second-rate and there were hundreds of younger sexier girls eager to join me for shopping.

We finally settled into Max's, a Philippine restaurant with a big expensive menu specializing in chicken. It would fit right at home in any American shopping mall. It was my choice, of course.

It was roughly 10pm and shortly after my meal, a wave of drowsiness overcame me. It was all I could do to keep from passing out at the table. At home, it was 7am, way past my normal bed time and now because the initial adrenaline of arriving had subsided compounded by a lazy disengaged day, jet lag had finally attacked furiously.

I explained that I had to return to the hotel and sleep and Ashley seemed surprised but enthusiastic. To her, lying in bed cuddling with a sleeping foreigner probably seemed like a bonus, though she had no idea just how passed out I was to become. She had to go back to her home early in the morning to finish packing and head to Manila for the flight to Camiguin.

Once I arrived at the hotel, I crashed as if I had just downed 10 shots of Jack Daniels with valium. I barely remember the walk and arriving, but I know I didn't lay awake in the bed longer than 30 seconds. I do recall a few short awakenings during the night with Ashley either fondling my dick or kissing my neck attempting to wake me up for some action, but I had no ability. I would wake up, throw my arms around her so she had to stop whatever she was doing and promptly pass out again.

It was her alarm at 8am that woke us both up. I was refreshed but she was now the one passed out. I knew she had to leave though, so I opened the curtains and took a shower.

"I don't want to go home now," Ashley whimpered to me while stretching out in the bed.

"Oh honey, I'm sorry," I said trying to be comforting, as I dropped my towel and slipped under the covers with her. There was no way I was letting this day go without entering her one last time.

She wrapped her arms around me and closed her eyes as my cock began to grow and poke into her belly. She let out a soft chuckle. Though she was tired and didn't seem in the mood, I began kissing her neck and slid my hand down to her ass and pulled her to me.

"I need to shower," she said. With that statement, I knew she was at least awake and willing, so I pulled back from her neck and began to kiss her to which she responded by grinding her pelvis into me.

"I just showered, you can suck my cock," I said in a demanding tone. I had learned that she enjoyed playing the submissive role in bed.

My stern voice seemed to activate her passion. She rolled me on to my back and shoved her tongue down my throat and then slowly made her way down. She stopped on my nipples for a little too long, so I placed my hand on her head and applied enough pressure that her mouth was on my dick a second later. She swallowed it.

After the long night of restful sleep, my libido was in overdrive and I decided to test just how submissive she liked to be. I brought both knees slowly toward my chest until my dick plopped out of her mouth. I waited to see what she would do and was not disappointed. She grabbed my cock with one hand and began to suck each nut in between licks and started massaging my asshole with her other hand.

She gently stroked me while sliding her tongue from the bottom of my balls all the way to the base of my dick. I decided to push it even further. I pulled my knees up a little more and pushed her head further down. She knew exactly what I was suggesting. She dropped my cock and put both hands on my butt cheeks spreading them slightly apart. In between she lodged her tongue in my ass as far as she could get it and then began flicking the opening slowly. I couldn't help but grab my now free cock and stroke it madly.

As I felt myself nearing orgasm, I thought I didn't want to cum on my belly. I do that quite regularly at home. I lowered my legs and Ashley again swallowed my dick like a starving child. I was lost in the moment and pushed her head down on my dick until the resistance of the back of her throat allowed no further pressure. She choked and two jets of saliva rocketed out the sides of her mouth. I gave her just enough respite to stop the gaging and again forced her head down. She was game and I no longer had to push as she grabbed the sides of my hips and forced herself down as long as she could between choking.

I didn't take long. As my orgasm erupted, my cum emptied straight down her throat. She was a trooper, she kept swallowing and forcing her head down and straining under the increased gagging reflex until I had completely relieved myself, became sensitive, and pulled her head off.

I leaned up grinning and looked straight into her eyes. She was betraying her emotions to be mixed. The tears of overexertion and redness in her cheeks indicated she had just endured an unpleasant experience, but the slight crook in the sides of her mouth told me she was proud and aroused at her service to me.

My dominating desire turned quickly to wanting to return the favor and I began to pull her body up to me with the intention of sitting her on my face. At first, she thought I simply wanted to hold her but when she discovered my intention she began to struggle.

"No Nathan! No! I haven't showered!"

I didn't care, in fact, I wanted to taste her day-old juices, but she would have none of it. She fought and pleaded until I gave up.

The type of personality Ashley had was completing itself in my mind. She was the kind of woman that didn't require massages, didn't require being pleasured. She was there to serve her man. She had never shown the slightest bit of aggression towards me or anyone else, she seemed to have a passive tendency. She was the perfect traditional wife. Though I wondered if she would remain that way after a year or so of marriage and especially marriage while living in a western country. Who is to say? It wasn't me who was going to find out. I wished I could have been more attracted to Ashley, she certainly deserved it.

She did shower, and by this time she was in a rush, running late to get home and get everything together and get on a bus to Manila. I thought that was better as I was sure it was going to be an emotional goodbye either way, but at least this way it wouldn't last long.

I accompanied her down the elevator, the whole time she was holding me tightly and digging her head into my chest not saying a word. As we arrived and walked toward the front door, I could see she was fighting back tears. I quickly signaled for the door man to bring up a trike.

At that point her tears erupted and she slobbered a big kiss on me and said, "I will miss you so much, please come back and see me."

My last memory of Ashley is sitting in the trike, her beautiful bare legs sticking out of her short dress and her hand outstretched as I let her go, tears flowing down her face, but with a big smile. She pulled her hand to her face and wiped one side and the trike was gone. I never saw her again.

CHAPTER 5

Lynn – the flashback

I had met Lynn two years previously. She was an above average bargirl on Don Juico, or Perimeter road in Angeles City. The local expats I meet tell me that is the only place to go for cheaper rates and better performance, but I enjoy frequenting the touristy and up-scale bars and clubs within walking distance to the nicer hotels near Walking Street. I suppose if you lived there, seeking out bargains would be required to keep from going broke and may become part of the fun as well. To me, it has always seemed a waste of time to frequent dive bars looking for a diamond among chunks of coal, when there are diamonds for sale up the street for only $20 more. Considering that I met Lynn on perimeter, perhaps I should have considered their advice a little earlier.

It was a late afternoon and I had recently met Jim. He drove me to his favorite bar and we sat down to have some drinks and watch the dancing by the more desperate of Angeles City's bargirls. Per Jim, this was the best kept bar on Perimeter and in fact it seemed well designed, new, and tastefully decorated, at least for a hole-in-the-wall bar which despite it's better materials could not hide the fact. The American owner influenced his opinion as well, I surmised[12].

Sitting opposite the small stage, we had the pleasure of 8 dancing Filipinas, and even though as far as I could tell we were the only patrons in the bar, they were already

---

[12] Mischief Bar, located in a small grouping of bars spaced out along Don Juico Ave.

dancing when we arrived. I wondered if this was due to the American management, as in most bars the girls will be sitting around until receiving a customer.

"Really Jim? You said this bar was the best out here," I joked after seeing the lineup. There were no girls on the stage I had interest in. It was a collection of young chubby girls, older single moms with leathery bellies, and otherwise hideously ugly girls.

"Not too good today, I agree," replied Jim. "Let's wait until the second lineup comes out though. San Mig?"

"There's a second lineup in this place?" For a small bar with no customers, it seemed strange there would be a ton of girls.

The second lineup came out before we even had our beers and I wondered if the first group was the no-customer group and the second was the real group. The new 8 girls were far better looking though still not all that interesting. Most of them didn't look happy to be there, didn't look interested in working, didn't make eye contact, and I wondered if they were forced to stand up there.

One girl seemed different though. Her smile drew my gaze instantly. Though older, around 28, she was skinny and attractive with fair skin unblemished by the common Filipino acne, scars, and stretch marks and seemed at ease with her position in the bar. Her hair was thick and wavy in the natural jet-black Asian color and hung to her mid-back, and looked like it was fixed by a professional hair stylist to get her ready for the runway.

"What do you think of her?" I asked Jim, pointing nonchalantly at the girl I just noticed, at which she turned her head to the side, smiled bigger and waved flirtatiously.

"She's been here awhile, not really my thing." To my friend, she was a complete turnoff, he liked the young and naïve. I, however, liked personality whether experienced or new.

With Jim's answer I took it as there was no real reason

not to buy her a few drinks, especially at the drink price of 80 pesos, so I waved her over. We had not gotten our own drinks yet, maybe this would speed the waitress up anyway. I don't think Jim was happy with my decision, he looked at me like the young rookie who had yet learned the proper way of picking up bargirls. I simply smiled back and shrugged.

She bounded over with a big smile on her face, plopped into the booth beside me and draped both her tiny legs over my left thigh with her knees resting comfortably on my crotch. "How are you, handsome? What's your name?"

After buying her drinks, my suspicions were confirmed. Her ability to turn me on was likely learned from years of observing and interacting with sex tourists. Her name was Lynn and she was originally from Mindanao.

Despite Angeles City's lifespan as a sex destination, it is oddly uncommon to find a truly experienced sex worker. There is a lot of churn in the industry, with girls getting bussed in from the province and either washing out due to bad experiences, finding a foreign husband, getting pregnant, or other reasons I probably am not aware of. Lynn was one of the few long-time workers. She was the main support for her two daughters and Filipino husband. The fact she was a single mother was hardly noticeable, another uncommon trait among bargirls, as usually stretch marks are quite visible. The openness about having a husband was a bit of a shocker to me and a turnoff, but after thinking about it for a moment, I decided I shouldn't worry too much about that, even if she were single, I likely wouldn't become interested in much more than one night.

Of course, it helped a ton that she was a bundle of joy, sexy as hell, and saying all the right things. "Oh, you look like Tom Cruise. I'm so lucky you picked me!" As she drank the few drinks that I bought for her, she began to hang on my shoulders and nibbled on my ear and even gave me a few big smooches. As I began to get hard, she used her hand and knee to make sure I never got soft again. For what amounted to $10, this was a far better strip club experience than I ever received for hundreds of dollars in the States.

Jim was nursing his San Mig Lites and seemed amused by the job the girl was doing on me. I would assume after living there for almost a decade, he was immune to those kinds of charms. I asked him why he didn't have a girl and even offered to buy another girl a drink if he got one but he declined. He said he didn't see anything he fancied and would look elsewhere. He didn't seem to mind that I probably wasn't going to join him for a bar hop.

For me, this girl was the exact thing I was looking for: fun, comfortable, sexy, and probably good in bed even if likely mechanical. I was soon to find out.

I paid the barfine of 1200 pesos[13], let Lynn get dressed, and then we all hung out and drank for a while in the bar with Jim. After 5 beers for me, 4 for her, the barfine, and tip for the waitress, my total bill at the bar came out to 2100 pesos (Less than $50 US). I can see why Jim and other expats like the bars out there. On Walking Street, the bill likely would have come to over 5000 pesos. How the girls make a living on perimeter and why a girl like Lynn would choose to work there instead of on Walking Street is a question I'll pretend I didn't think of and instead just take advantage of the situation. Lynn did mention that the barfine wasn't much and she hoped to get a tip. *Yep, professional.*

---

[13] Barfine up to 1,800 pesos as of this writing.

Don't call crying screaming drunk bargirls to your table for a drink.

In the middle of our little party, we were interrupted by a dancer screaming on stage. She wasn't screaming at anyone, maybe herself or her imaginary friend. She just kind of went nuts suddenly. It was too early in the evening to be wasted but she seemed that way to me. I'd love to know what she was screaming but she inconsiderately did her screaming in Tagalog.

"Ohhh geez!" laughed Lynn. "Excuse please one moment."

Lynn went to the stage and put her arm around the crazy girl who had now slumped down on her knees and was letting the tears flow. It occurred to me that Lynn and she were easily the best-looking girls in the club, and wait, was that a little more than a sensitive friendly hug I was seeing?

It seemed Lynn was mostly laughing and perhaps even ridiculing her in Tagalog, in between little temper tantrums and slapping away of hands. Jim and I were discussing the situation and enjoying the show and we came to the simple conclusion that she was drunk and jealous that I was having her girlfriend. *Obviously.* With each passing moment, we both started to believe Lynn and this girl shared the bed a time or two. Or maybe we were horny men in a bar wanting to believe that? Only one way to find out.

I went up to the stage and invited Lynn to bring her over to our table and I'd buy her a drink. Lynn, who had been laughing and doing her best to calm down the situation, did not look too pleased with that idea, but of course it was too late, a smile came instantly to the tearful eyed girl and she got up and walked over to the table. A drink will cheer up anyone.

"This is my girlfriend, Jen," said Lynn.

"Girlfriend, as in you know?" I asked. "Aren't you married?"

"Oh, it's ok, I have my girlfriends."

Jen had obviously been downing shots of rum. I could smell it as if she had soaked in it. "My girl!" she said hearing the conversation. "Hey! You take us both! You love it!"

"No, you're too drunk," Lynn laughed and threw her arms around her. I certainly agreed with her, she was too drunk and I was repulsed by her smell and attitude. Lynn should be able to do better.

"I good blowjob. You try!" Jen said to me and put her hands on my crotch. She couldn't find what she was looking for though. "Try Try Try Try." She began patting my crotch, as if that would help.

In a flash so I could do nothing to stop it, she climbed over me and straight punched Jim in the dick yelling, "Hey you, I give you blowjob!"

Jim calmly stated, "The fuck you will."

I lifted myself while holding her to keep her from flopping in the floor and scooted her off me. As she slid her face down to my crotch she began plowing her nose forcefully into me. It was not arousing in the least. It was as if a bag lady was attempting to prop her rum-stricken body upright by latching her nostrils onto my cock.

Lynn raised her voice saying something to her in Tagalog and Jen backed away from me. I believe Lynn could feel my annoyance at her girlfriend who had ruined our nice little party. Or did I ruin it? I did call her over, didn't I? Lesson learned on dealing with drunk bargirls: Don't call crying screaming drunk bargirls to your table for a drink.

Lynn was now screaming at her in Tagalog and I retreated to conversing with Jim.

"So, have you ever had a threesome?" Jim asked me.

"Not really. One time I brought two girls to my room

but they just hustled me for more money and I threw them out," I answered referring to one experience I had with American call-girls long ago. "What about you?"

"Oh sure."

"And?" I asked him truly wanting to hear.

"I went crazy when I first moved here, I've probably had more threesomes than you've had girls," he replied snickering. "I've never really had a bad threesome, not like yours anyway. Lynn and her girlfriend might be fun, though I'd definitely pick another night."

Jim did get me thinking at least, though I was utterly disgusted by Jen. It wasn't happening with her any night for any price.

"Hey you! Take me too!" slurred Jen at me. And with that Lynn stood up and started dragging Jen away from the table. The process of removing Jen took a good five minutes and Jim and I enjoyed the little cat fight playing out in the middle of the bar on Perimeter Road in Angeles City, Philippines. Never short of experiences.

Eventually, Lynn and I said our goodbyes to Jim and piled into one of Angeles City's trikes, which are easily some of the smallest in the Philippines. In places like Cebu and especially Dumaguete, the trikes are huge. Of course, then they compensate by piling as many as 10 people in them, so I guess it doesn't really matter the size of them. You are going to fit in a space that you can fit in.

Lynn was relaxed, and though not the aggressive flirty girl from before I barfined her still carried a smile and charming personality as we rode toward the Pacific Breeze. At least she was not the kind of career happy-hooker that goes cold as soon as the sale can no longer be retracted, although I wasn't hearing anything more like I was her "Tom Cruise." Oh well.

"So, what was all that about at the bar with the other girl?" I asked Lynn.

Lynn let out a little giggle and said, "She's just upset

about her boyfriend."

"Boyfriend? Aren't you two...?"

"So?" said Lynn breaking into another amusing giggle.

I smiled and remembered just how conservative I was for a sex tourist.

"I like girls a lot, but I'm not lesbian. She's not either," Lynn said.

"Well, you kind of are," I asserted.

"No! Lesbians only like girls. I like men more, girls are just fun."

I left it at that.

There was a little foreplay and polite conversation in the room but it was basically straight to the shower and straight to work on the oral sex... that is what I like about experienced girls, I don't have to ask or hint around, she already knows what to do. As her hands and tongue work my cock into submission, I slowly glide back on the bed. Once I lay down, she swallows my dick with as much effort as she can muster and begins a fast head bobbing blowjob, interrupted occasionally when she'd have to deal with her enormous, but beautiful pile of hair laid to the side of one of my thighs.

At one moment, I lift my head and look down at her to find her eyes staring straight into mine as if she knew that look was coming. At that point, she lifts her head off my cock slowly with her tongue sticking out and a small dribble of spit running between her tongue and the tip of my dick. With that she begins sliding her body up with little nibbles on my belly and chest, while her hair smothers one side of my torso. With one arm she reaches for the condom on the table and with the other she is holding my neck to help the pressure of lips on my cheek and ear.

With some skill, she keeps her pussy as close as possible to my dick without giving me any hope that I'd be able to slide it in without that condom, not that it was my intention anyway. With her level of experience, if she wasn't using condoms, it would be on the level of Russian Roulette to go unprotected.

Sex with Lynn was pretty standard, though that is to be expected with experienced sex workers. That said, it was good. She used her hands over my body in a way that kept me engaged, didn't rush me, and acted like she was having fun. And to that end, I think she was having a little fun. She didn't seem to be hiding any displeasure, at least.

The most memorable aspect of our time in the bed was her hair draping over me as she rode on my cock. Though her body was nothing special in terms of bargirls, her hair was full and elegant, soft and smelled like mangoes. It felt like I was fucking a well-to-do rich Asian who paid massive sums of money to maintain her hair style.

In spite of her quick exit after my being finished (she told me at the bar she was short time only), she somehow ended up on my Facebook. While I'm unopposed to keeping in contact with girls I buy sex from, it happens at dinner on the second barfine or in the morning after a great night when I want to see them again. I still can't recall how she ended up on my friends list, though later on my next trip, it would turn out to precipitate one of the greatest nights of sex I've ever had. But I'll get to that, still a ton of girls to go in the meantime...

CHAPTER 6

The new girl from Perimeter

Jet lag still a hurdle to my days in Angeles, I was up at 6am the following day after Ashley with nothing to do. Early morning can be a boring time in Angeles, especially if the weather isn't good and just laying around at the pool is not an option. After breakfast and flirting with the charming girls at the Central Park restaurant (totally off limits), I wasted time on the Internet in my room waiting for the noon hour.

Around noon is when some of the bars start to open, especially the ones out on Perimeter. I had only made one trip to Perimeter in my life and that was at the behest of Jim. This time, I thought I'd take a trip down there and walk up the strip to the Clarkton Hotel.

I jumped in a trike and landed at the same bar I had met Lynn. I handed the driver 100 pesos and started to walk away as he said "150! 150!" This was a first for me. I hadn't been all that happy when the price jumped to 100 pesos, and here's this guy yelling at me for a 150 price. I simply answered, "If you wanted 150, you should have told me before I got in." He threw a miniature, and slightly cute, little fit as I walked into the bar.

There were no Lynn's in there on this trip. In fact, I was a disheartened, the talent was abysmal. I'm not sure if my expectations were elevated due to the one trip I had there previously, and this was more average or if I caught them on a bad day. I don't expect that the hour of the day had much to do with it, as is the case with most sex destinations, there are plenty of attractive girls that like working early and avoiding the whole night scene.

68

Well, there are plenty of bars around on perimeter, so I started barhopping toward the Clarkton Hotel.

With Clarkton in sight, I saw the little strip of bars I'd heard of flanking the hotel in the direction of Fields Avenue. My first stop was in Orange bar and I was instantly more satisfied with the level of talent. Although prettier and younger, they seemed a little lazy. The bar was of the stage-in-the-middle variety with booths lining the outer walls, and the girls were sitting and laying around like a pack of Lions lounging on a hot day in the Sahara.

One lone customer was busy fondling two of the girls in the corner and I settled myself opposite him and waited for the glances from the girls who were eager to work. And I waited...

When stepping into a bar packed with girls and no customers, I tend to get swamped. It's practically an art form sifting through the aggressive girls to find the girl of my dreams for the night, but this bar seemed quite lethargic. At least the waitress came over to hand me a San Mig Lite.

I wasn't even getting looks, what the hell was going on here? I saw at least a dozen girls laying around doing nothing, or texting, or doing nothing. This was practically out of the twilight zone; did I somehow slip in unnoticed? Or perhaps this bar usually gets an Asian clientele and my white face was a turnoff. Either way, there were a couple girls who I thought were cute, so I called the waitress to get them over. To my satisfaction, the lumps on the stage did in fact move when the waitress pointed them my way. Movement, though not necessarily a requirement for what I was interested in purchasing, would help the enjoyment of it.

The girls we'll call Beth and Diana, because I forgot both their names within minutes after being out of their presence. One because I didn't like her much and the other because she didn't like me much. Diana was a seasoned Angeles City vet. I could tell by her first glance at me. It was very business oriented and relaxed. She was cute, a single mother obviously but very subtle stretch marks and still a hot body. Beth, would fall under the same description for her body, but totally opposite in her demeanor. My first eye contact with her screamed new girl.

Ladies' drinks were fairly expensive in this perimeter bar at 200 pesos each, and not having the typical two price choice. That sealed the deal for me that regardless of whether I liked these girls, there would be only one drink. Diana was fun, the typical Filipina bar worker. Smiling and laughing and rubbing herself on me for about $5US, this is why I come to Angeles City. Beth was just adorable... in the cute innocent way. I don't necessarily search for new girls, I search for personality and while Diana was charming, there was nothing special about it. In fact, it was mechanical and obvious. I'm sure she would have been great fun in bed, but my draw was to Beth.

When in doubt, don't take new girls.

Beth was not schmoozing me like Diana. She seemed interested but like all new girls was too shy to engage me. She was waiting on me to make the move. She was sitting next to me with her legs and arms crossed. She was about 21 years old and judging by her very subtle stretch marks on her hip and a touch of baby fat around her belly button, had just given birth. I'm sure she was there for that reason. She had blonde highlights and was wearing a two-piece black dress allowing plenty of space to run my hands around her lower back and latch onto her opposite thigh. She gently slid toward me and smiled.

"How long have you been working here?" I asked.

The coy reaction as she answered "two weeks" was a

70

little confusing to me. I usually assume two weeks is an honest answer. When a bargirl will lie about how long she has worked, it is because they don't want to admit they have been working in the industry for years. An answer of two to six months can mean anything from two months to five years. But an experienced worker just can't fake two weeks and won't attempt a lie that big. I would soon discover that while it wasn't a lie, her reaction to the question indicated a total lack of experience in answering it. She was simply not used to explaining how long she'd been selling herself for sex.

As their drinks dwindled and I enjoyed myself playing with the overly aggressive Diana while copping feels of the bashful Beth, my intentions for the afternoon became clear. I was not interested in Diana at all and I was developing quite the lust for Beth. When the time came to buy more drinks, I announced, "Well, I don't really want to buy any more drinks, but I'd love to take one of you out of here."

"I can't barfine right now," Diana announced, making everything easy for me. The two of them started talking to each other in Tagalog with the occasional giggles and glances at me, and whatever they were saying was obviously in prep to send Beth home with me, which is what I preferred anyway.

"She wants to go but she's shy," Diana announced finally.

"I'm a nice guy, and I won't keep you long." I wasn't really sure if that was what she wanted, but a confirmation that she'd barfine with me was quickly announced.

Beth removed herself to change after I handed over 2000 pesos, and I continued my rubbing with Diana while waiting. I tried to fish Diana for a little more information on Beth but all I really got was, "Oh, she's new girl." *Yea, thanks for that bombshell.*

When Beth reappeared wearing the standard jean

shorts + tight sleeveless cotton shirt with flip-flops, she looked borderline miserable from nervousness. It seemed at that point that I was one of her first barfines, and that she wasn't working in that bar at all because she wanted to be. It was simply something she had to do and get through. I was regretting my decision already. When in doubt, don't take new girls.

I took her directly to my room at Central Park and she walked in gingerly and placed her phone on the nightstand by the bed and looked around. I laid down on the bed and invited her to join me. My goal was to make her more comfortable and to find just how new she was. As she lay facing me with her arm casually draped on my shoulder, I begin to fish out her situation. It was mostly as I surmised in the bar. She was from a poor family in Leyte and she had gotten pregnant from a Filipino who promptly abandoned her.

This is a common story right down to the province. Often girls will come at the urging of another girl in her family who made it big in Manila or Angeles, but many of them are just not suited to the life. Beth definitely fell into that category.

Furthering our conversation, I discovered her nervousness arose mostly from me being her first white customer. She had been busy for her first two weeks but so far had turned down customers other than Japanese and Korean. Unusual for Filipinas, she really didn't seem too impressed with Westerners, and she was worried about the size of my cock. When girls say that, I typically assume it's their way of asking me not to pound the hell out of them, but Beth was simply yet to find out that her pussy would expand for any size dick. Perhaps the little giggling conversation in the bar was Diana telling her that my cock wasn't that big?

Fast-forward 15 minutes, two separate showers, and we are naked under the covers kissing. She has lightened up and is having a bit of fun by now. I give myself props for being able to calm girls in this situation... call it experience and preferring not to feel like I'm raping them. I didn't bother asking for a blowjob, it probably wouldn't have been good even if she was willing. When it was time, I grabbed a condom, moved between her legs and penetrated her gently. It was a wonderful sight watching myself enter between the thin sexy hips she had. I focused on her legs instead of the little bit of baby fat she had on her stomach. Regardless of that, the girl had good genes. She could probably pop out babies every year for 10 years and still hold a nice frame.

Even though I was being extra careful, she was a little squirmy and uncomfortable with some lip biting and groans of displeasure. After a couple minutes I pulled out and lay back down beside her smiling and comforting her that I wouldn't be mad. She smiled back and began to apologize saying that she'd like to just wait a bit. That was fine with me and I took off the condom and prepared for a little cuddling and more talking.

But it wasn't talking I'd get. She laid her head on my pillow, closed her eyes and nudged her face under my cheek. Then, she reached both her hands down and began massaging my dick. This was quite nice and it was just fine with me that we'd be skipping more conversation. Even though she was new and not right for this kind of work, she knew the job she was there to do. The massages got faster and she moved her body into me and lifted her knee on top of my hip so I was pointing towards her pussy again.

"Let's try without a condom," she said to me and started to roll back and pull me on top of her. I flinched at first. Since my encounter in Manila, I had been a little ashamed of myself, but in reality I didn't expect the situation to happen again, so I had not made any sort of vow with myself to wear condoms. Sex workers generally ask for condoms so it's not a decision I have to make. In this instance, I didn't debate with myself too long. New girl two weeks from the province, why should I worry about this?

I slid inside her to find a soft moist tight vagina enveloping me. The difference between this intercourse and the previous with the condom was profound. It seemed much better for her as well, so any desire I may have had to stop and put one on was gone. I finished quickly and managed to pull out and release on the bed. This wasn't much of a problem for me, I have no interest in knocking up a poverty-stricken girl from the Philippines. Plus, it would limit her new career choice to just a few months.

Afterward, I scolded her about wearing condoms. Although a little hypocritical of me, it was still something she should hear. I warned her that most men will not be as courteous as I was for pulling out and that if she continued to not wear condoms, she would quickly contract some form of STD, which I'm not even sure she understood what an STD was. Oh well, this was just the way I lived with myself for not using one.

Afterward, her mood changed back to the shameful girl who walked out from the back of the club after changing, and she was ready to leave. That was fine, I was ready for her to leave as well. Since I was hungry, I walked her out of the hotel and down the street trying to have some sort of small talk with her. She seemed quite disgusted by me then. Was it the condom talk? I don't know, maybe she was simply ashamed of having another one-night stand, or another afternoon sexual romp rather.

"Where are you going?" she asked, obviously annoyed I was still in her company.

"Oh, I'm going this way, bye bye," and with that we parted and I headed to Tequila Reef to grab some fatty Mexican food in the middle of Angeles City, Philippines.

CHAPTER 7

The Tequila Reef Wingmen

Financially, sex tourists vary widely. On one end of the scale are the extremely cheap travelers who will stay in the lower end hotels with hard foam mattresses in tiny rooms, eat street food, and aggressively negotiate with the girls they take home. On the other end are the weekend millionaires who bring their western salaries to Angeles once or twice a year and intend on spending every dime in their bank accounts on the prettiest girls and the nicest rooms. We all lean in one direction.

Allen was the former and John the latter. I had met John for a moment in Lollipop when I was barhopping. When I walked through the doors into Tequila Reef, our eyes locked and we exchanged the "Hey man, how'd the other night end up for you?" conversations that only sex tourists really can do, and I invited myself to their table.

John was about 55 and some sort of successful farm worker from Illinois. Allen, his tightwad friend (or Kuripot as the girls would say), was a retired accountant from Los Angeles, about 60 years old who was obviously an Angeles City regular. Their looks also fit them perfectly. John was a heavy-set tall guy who looked like he'd worked and played and ate well his whole life. Allen, on the other hand, was a smaller lean guy that looked like he ate salad and salmon every day for 60 years. After exchanging some introductions and pleasantries, I liked them both immediately.

"HOW'S THAT YOUNG ASIAN PUSSY TREATING YOU?" John asked with a booming voice that caused a few heads to turn.

A big smile came to my face with part of me thinking how nice it must be to have that lack of shame and the other part of me loving where I am. Angeles City is anything but short of characters.

"Pretty standard so far this trip, haven't fell in love, haven't had my brains fucked out either, except that for some strange reason so far I haven't been using condoms. I don't really know why. They have just ended up not on.

"My first girl in Manila had a condom sitting on the bed and she just climbed on without it," I explained. "And I'm lying there thinking, 'ah fuck it.'"

Allen burst out into laughter, "That sounds familiar! Ah man, I didn't wear condoms for years when I first started coming here." As he told the story, I learned he started coming to Angeles City 10 years ago at the age of 50 after getting a divorce and having his tubes clipped. His reasoning was that he couldn't get them pregnant and he was old enough that he wasn't too worried about contracting anything serious.

"Did you ever get an STD?" I asked, of course wondering a little for myself by this point.

"Oh, all the time. There is some strain of chlamydia around here that they all have. I got gonorrhea one time from this little spinner[14] out on Perimeter who just wouldn't hear it. I wonder how many men she gave it to. I tell you, gonorrhea is no fun at all, but there is a one-armed Doc here that can fix you right up."

"A one-armed Doc?" asked John.

"As in, only one arm. He does just fine, even showed me the little critters in the scum oozing from my dick under a microscope. That's medical service for you. What are you worried about anyway? You family man!" answered Allen.

"Family man?" At first, I thought he must have a

---

[14] Spinner – Term used for smaller girls. You know… spin them around on your dick… get the image?

family back home and be sneaking out on them but come to find out he was engaged to a bargirl from Angeles City and was there waiting for her papers to go through to take her back to Illinois. He said he wasn't allowed to sleep with any more girls in Angeles, but that barhopping and a bit of fun was ok.

"Speaking of barhopping, are we about done here?" Allen pleaded with us. Out of the two, John was far more laid back than Allen. I might even characterize Allen as a control freak.

I was tired by then due to jet lag, even though it was only 6pm. I may have even skipped barhopping completely had I not been traveling alone. Traveling alone makes the offer of wingmen too important to pass up.

It seemed like it would take a while before we left Tequila Reef though. John was busy flirting and joking with one of the waitresses, who would practically break down into a hysteric every time she walked by. I tried to do the flirting thing but I'm simply not good at it.

Angeles City is full of hot women, whether it be in the bars, the streets, waitresses or front desk clerks. I've never attempted to pick up any of the women outside the bars in Angeles, I figure they get hit on all the time and truly what's the point? I'm there to have sex with whores. If I wanted to pick up normal girls, I'd go elsewhere, such as Boracay. Chasing a front desk girl or waitress seems like it would just cut into barhopping and fucking. Though if you ask Allen about it, he'll give you a very frank answer, "Every woman in Angeles City is a whore."

I believe Allen was mostly sitting at the table arguing with himself whether to be patient. He had some very laid out plans and we were interfering with them. As I got to know them both over the course of the trip, I found that this odd duo from America met about five years previous at the airport in Manila heading to Angeles. They shared a cab and had been good friends ever since.

After a few more beers had been downed, John leaned into me and lowered his voice slightly. I say slightly, but with John it was more like instead of the whole restaurant being able to hang on his every word, it was merely every table next to us.

"Here is what I used to do about condoms. I would never say anything about them and just continue like they didn't exist. If by the time I had my dick next to her pussy, she still had not uttered one word about it, I would get up and put on a condom. I ain't fucking some bargirl that has had every dick in the world in her without bagging up."

I was a little confused. Seems like that would entail always using condoms.

"I don't get it, so what would you do when she asked you to wear one?"

"I wouldn't."

Allen nearly spilt his drink. "You really think that would matter? Every guy running around here with the clap is fucking them all without condoms and it doesn't matter what they say."

"No, but it helps my odds a bit," John replied confidently.

I was still a little confused. "So, how did you get them to not use a condom?"

"Oh, most of them don't really care. Just keep going like you didn't hear them. For the ones that fight a little, just tell them you don't like condoms. Make up some stupid excuse. I like the 'my dick is too big, it will hurt' excuse. If they still fight, offer them more pesos. But, I've never had to give them more money and I've only had one girl completely refuse no matter what and I had to actually put a condom on."

I was thinking about all this. It is certainly something I would never be able to do. If they asked me to put a condom on, I'd put one on. So, in John's mind, if I only wore condoms with the girls that required me to but never used a condom with girls that didn't mention them, I'd be just asking for an STD. John is also quite charming and has a way with people and I'm sure women as well. He could likely talk them into not using a condom and make them happy about it in the process.

"Allen, what would you do if they asked you to wear a condom?" I turned and asked.

"As I said, I never wore a condom for a long time, now I always do. Just call it a change of heart after one too many times pissing razor blades."

I noticed a bargirl with her boyfriend at the next table with a look of disgust toward John and I thought, 'I take it you weren't the one that fought him until he put one on.'

Much to Allen's delight, we finally peeled away from our table at Tequila Reef. John was borderline wasted, I was way tipsier than I like to be so early, and Allen's two whole beers had no effect on him. It's nice that we had a designated driver.

We didn't really go far though as John made a beeline for Crystal Palace right across the small backroad.

"He likes these expensive places," Allen said to me.

Crystal Palace is one of the nicer bars on Walking Street with a big stage, lots of girls, plush seats, and a generally laid-back atmosphere. It is connected to the even nicer but more pretentious Dollhouse Bar which exits on the other side of the building. When the three of us entered, the bar had few customers having just opened, and the stage was packed with girls. While Allen and I grabbed a booth near the door, John staggered up to the stage yelling, "Hey ladies, don't worry, I'm here!" much to the pleasure of the bored looking dancers.

As Allen and I ordered beers and began a methodical

examination of the girls on display, John really knew how to live it up. With a bundle of 20-peso notes, he was doing his own type of examination: of asses and nipples. With every 20-peso note he handed out, he required a close up view and a gentle pat or squeeze. I was impressed at his non-discriminatory handouts. Whether young or old, slim or fat, beautiful or butt-ugly, he patted or squeezed and supplied a 20.

The girls were having quite the time, especially one obviously more experienced girl who was dragging some of the newer girls up to receive their pat and 20 pesos. Allen and I found it funny that girls who chose to be in the sex business might find exposing their tits for a nipple squeeze at the bar to be too embarrassing.

"Do you ever join him in handing out 20's?" I asked Allen.

"Oh, dear God no. He's just throwing away money. He likes all this, I could care less about, I just pick out a girl and take her to the hotel," replied Allen.

"So why do you hang out with him?" was my real question.

"John is an amazing wingman to have. For all his antics, he knows how to stay out of trouble and how to keep me out of trouble. It's also easier to have fun without spending money if you have someone next to you who is. I'll let him keep all the girls happy in the bar, while I make them happy in the hotel room. Although, I suspect he makes them happier in the hotel as well."

With that I decided to join John up on stage and pass out some 20s for myself. I figured I'd up the ante and stuff the 20s down the fronts of their panties.

"Check this one out…" said John as I sat down. He took another 20-peso bill out and motioned to one really pretty young girl on the stage, who came over with a pleasant innocent smile and squatted down to receive her pat on the ass and 20 pesos.

I pulled out my own 20 and motioned to her and with some well portrayed charades managed to communicate that I wanted her to drop to her knees in front of me and lower her panties so I could stuff the 20 in. As I reached in, I made sure to caress her clit with my index finger. She didn't seem to mind one bit.

"Ha ha ha, that's the way, get in there," John laughed, and he added the new move to his repertoire.

A mere 15 minutes later, I had gone through 500 pesos and got not much more for it than a couple pussy grabs. John may have gone through 2000, but he was certainly the life of the bar. The girls were all smiling and screaming, and many had come down to stroke his crotch, give him massages, and other such things strippers do to paying customers. I had enough though, I guess I lean more towards Allen's style. I rejoined him and John soon followed me.

"Let's see what's happening at Dollhouse!" barked the even more inebriated John.

"Oh great, you going to send them all to college in there?" mocked Allen.

We walked through the small entranceway in Dollhouse and encountered a lively scene. There were more customers, more girls, and in my opinion far more pretty girls. My eyes were drawn quickly to a fair-skinned slim beauty with long black hair and Chinese facial features. Her butt had a moderate bubble and she had medium sized perky tits giving her a nearly supermodel appearance while dancing on stage. This was the feature group and she was by far the most beautiful.

John did not attempt his 20-peso bill game on the featured dancers and we three slid into a booth on the side of the round stage.

"My God, she's amazing!" I exclaimed, unable to keep my eyes off the beauty I had seen.

"Call her over," said Allen. "Too rich for my blood

though. You'll pay four thousand pesos and get half the service as you would for two thousand pesos at a different bar."

He's right of course, and I knew that already. Though, for me, the problem in taking her out was not so much in the price I'd pay or the service I'd get, it's that she was just too beautiful for me. The reason I'm there in the first place is because I'm shy and nervous around women. While the exchange of funds will reduce my nervousness in most cases, when dealing with women who are way out of my league, I still get nervous, and being nervous usually means not having fun.

"I need some pussy!" yelled John, and got up and walked to the edge of the stage that a rope was attached to. He took the rope off and yanked on it until hundreds of little ping pong balls dropped on stage. The girls, who had now changed back from the feature group, all dropped to the floor and began fighting over the little balls. I looked up at the bucket to discover John had just paid 4000 pesos for the privilege of watching semi-naked girls scrambled like animals for little balls that represented 20 pesos each.

It did serve one very convenient purpose. Within 5 minutes, our booth was full of bouncing giggling sexy young girls. For the next hour, the drinks flowed and the ladies swooned. John was spending money like he had unlimited funds and Allen and I were enjoying the free ride. I can see why Allen likes to hang out with John and as the night wore on, I began to understand John's desire to keep him around. As the bills piled up in the wooden cylinder[15] on our table, Allen kept a close eye on each one and often questioned the bill, though each time it was merely that he had not noticed some expenditure John

---

[15] In virtually every bar and some restaurants in Angeles City (and in most of the Philippines), tickets are supplied as you place your orders and left on your table in some kind of holder. It is customary to never be asked to pay until you offer it up yourself.

made.

Allen got to ride the coattails of the weekend millionaire. John got to spend carefree while his buddy made sure he wasn't ripped off. Their partnership in barhopping now made a little sense. Seems as though Allen got the better end of the deal though – as I'm sure he did with everything in life.

CHAPTER 8

The Runout and the Beauty

Buying sex can be a very simple thing. You see the girl you'd like to have sex with, pay her fee, take her to your hotel room and have sex with her. Unfortunately, with any service paid for and provided by other people, there is a range of quality. Naturally, a very beautiful bargirl will develop the habit of not working hard to please her customers as her beauty alone accomplishes it. They can simply get in bed, lay there, and let the customer do the work. He will likely be fully aroused simply because of what he sees before him. Finding a truly beautiful working girl that also goes to great lengths to make sure her customer enjoys his time is a difficult prospect. It is a search I don't put much effort in.

On the other hand, for most of us, we'd simply never have the gratification of taking a sincerely beautiful woman into bed if we were not paying her to join us. For that reason, I strive to find at least one supermodel-level bargirl per trip to enjoy and assume she might simply lay there, or have an attitude, or try to get out of having sex altogether. Of course, experiences such as those could happen with any bargirl, but the likelihood of it seems directly proportional to her beauty.

Only buy drinks for girls you are actually interested in, don't be charity.

"I'm Star, what's your name?" asked the moderately attractive girl who had joined our booth after John attempted to bring half the bar over.

"Star? Is that your real name?" I asked thinking I'd never quite heard a name like that from a Filipina, or for that matter anywhere besides TV.

"Yes, see!" she said pointing to her identification trifecta. I decided to leave it alone, as I'm sure she had that conversation every night.

"My parents were hippies," she added giggling.

"You poor thing."

Star seemed to me a very average girl for Dollhouse. If perhaps I had found her in another bar, she would have compared better and I would have liked her more, but as it was, I just wasn't all that interested. Since she was in our booth having a good time, I went ahead and bought her a drink. Allen, on the other hand, turned down every girl saying he wasn't interested. There is a lesson here. Only buy drinks for girls you are actually interested in, don't be charity.

"Oh, thank you honey!" screamed Star as I agreed to the drink purchase. "Do you mind if I invite my friend over? She's really pretty."

"Is she prettier than you?" I flirted.

At that point, I was lost in the atmosphere of our booth and very drunk so when the supermodel I had noticed on stage when we first walked in appeared next to Star, I was in shock. In fact, I felt the subtle emergence of the kind of tension a man gets when in the company of a remarkable woman he has yet to become acquainted with.

She had the kind of presence that affects everyone around her. Her movements were graceful and effortless. She placed her hand on the booth halfway behind Star's shoulder blades and glided her body delicately into the booth. She moved in a way that if she was at a 5-star hotel in New York City, she would not seem out of place. The soft smile and sassy facial expression however gave away her conceited personality. She knew how beautiful she was.

I feigned disinterest and introduced myself as if I was only being polite. "Hello, I'm Nathan."

"Hi Nathan, I'm Marian," she said offering her hand to me. Even the feel of her hand was high class. Soft palms, skinny fingers, perfectly manicured nails, and a light touch had me wondering if I had been transported to a high-class Manila night club.

As I peered into her eyes, I noticed they were blue, and obviously, contacts. That along with her straight black hair, tasteful white makeup, and northern Asian facial characteristics distinguished her from all the other girls I'd seen in Angeles City.

"Hey! You buy her drink?" barked the waitress thankfully snapping me out of my trance.

"Yes, of course!" I replied not hesitating.

I could feel Allen nudging me from behind. "You are absolutely right, she is stunning. If you don't take her, I might," he said into my ear.

While a more confident sex tourist might start throwing attention directly to Marian, I could not bring myself to engage her. It's as if I was terrified of this beautiful Angeles City bargirl. So instead I directed my conversation to both Star and her.

"How long have you two been working here?" I started with the tedious question.

"Six months," said Star.

"Two years," said Marian.

It surprised me Marian had been working there as a dancer that long. It seemed she could have had her choice of rich foreigners by now. She did appear to be a few years older than Star, I'd guess 25.

"So, what are you guys doing tonight? Just drinking? Partying?" asked Star.

"Mostly drinking," I answered as that did seem to be what we were doing. At least that is what John and I were doing. Allen was still sipping his beers. Later, as I got to

86

know him better, I often wondered if he sipped beer only because he didn't want to spend the money to buy more.

"Take us to High Sol[16]?" pleaded Star.

"Both of you?"

"Yes! Uh huh!" they answered in unison.

I laughed out loud. "You think I'm rich?"

"Uh huh!" they nodded their head.

I laughed back, but I was beginning to fall into a drunken binge where money becomes less important. It is a state I abhor; especially when in foreign countries. If things kept going as they were, it is possible I could be breaking out some sort of dorky disco dance at High Society trying to act the pimp with one very average bargirl and her stunning friend.

"I didn't peg you to be the big spender," said Allen to me.

Another hour had passed with John throwing money around to different girls in Dollhouse. I believe he would not have been satisfied until every girl in the bar had sat on his lap. And although the destination for most of my money rested in the two girls, Star and Marian, I had joined him in the disposal of funds. Chicken wings, shots, drinks, ping pong balls, confetti poppers, you name it. Within just a couple hours, I had managed to spend 5,000 pesos and John was probably north of 20,000. It's fine, I'm on vacation, I kept assuring myself.

"Gents," said John. "I need to go to the hotel and fuck my wife!" A chorus of laughter erupted from the girls in the booth. Allen, seeing no reason to stay at Dollhouse, also announced his departure. I was stuck though, I was

---

[16] "High Sol" – How the girls refer to High Society, the night club on Walking Street.

going to take one of the girls out. I had invested so much getting them comfortable with me, it seemed absurd to look elsewhere.

For reasons I do not fully understand, I decided that I would barfine Star that night and then come back some other day when I was sober and not jet lagged to barfine Marian. Maybe that was the real reason, or maybe I was just scared to take her at all. What would I do with a girl like her? She seemed too elegant to take to my hotel and treat like a whore.

And Star was fine. At least she would be for a short session right before I passed out. I did my normal routine of letting her know she could leave right after sex and she seemed happy with that as well as being happy about being barfined at all. So, what happened next surprised me.

Don't leave a bargirl alone after you've paid but before you've consummated the deal.

We went straight to my room on the 9th floor of Central Park and when I inserted my keycard into the door, it did not work. I asked her if she wanted to come down to the lobby with me or wait there and she said she would wait. I quickly got into the elevator, went downstairs to rekey the card and after a short 2 minutes, I was exiting the elevator back on the 9th floor to which I discovered an absent Star. I looked around the floor, went down to the lobby to check if she came down but after 5 minutes of waiting and searching concluded that she took the opportunity to run out on me.

This was my first run out ever in my sex tourist career. I'd heard of it happening, but thought it was a rare occurrence that only happened to assholes or pigs. I was a little drunk but still very respectful as usual. I'm sure her motivations had little to do with me, or perhaps she thought I was too nice or too inexperienced to return to the bar to demand my money back. She hoped she could receive the barfine money without having to do the deed? The lesson here is obvious: Don't leave a bargirl alone after you've paid but before you've consummated the deal.

Well, I'm not inexperienced and not so tired that I'd just go into my room and pass out. I headed straight back to Dollhouse. As I approached the back of the stage scanning the room for who to talk to, Marian noticed me where she was waiting for the next line up. "Nathan, what's wrong? Where is Star?"

"I don't know, she disappeared on me, where is the Mama-san?" I asked her.

"Oh my God, she did what? Why would she do that?" Marian exclaimed with a look of actual surprise on her face. Her reaction satisfied me that it wasn't some sort of plan between the two.

"Wait here," and with that she glided down off the steps and floated away towards the back.

In total contrast, I stumbled over to the nearest empty booth and crashed like the drunken slob ready to pass out that I was. The waitress who had been so rewarded by our presence earlier was quick to show up and offer me another beer. At that point, why not have another?

I had not even received the beer when Marian showed up with two mama-sans. One of them I had met earlier when I paid the barfine and the other seemed to have more authority over matters. In any event, it seemed like something they were used to dealing with, having an almost scripted dialogue with me.

I was told that I could not have the money back, but that I could pick a new girl. This surprised me, as from all the stories I'd heard of run outs, the bars would absolutely refund the money. At first, I began to protest, even though there was an obvious choice for me - a choice that I probably should have made in the first place.

Marian was standing next to the senior mama-san avoiding eye contact with me. I wasn't sure if it was an attempt to avoid being barfined or simply a sort of embarrassment that she was about to be the second choice. Though I assumed she knew the choice that was about to be posed to me and if she did not want to receive the already paid moneys, she would have made herself scarce.

"Marian, would you like to go with me?" I asked confidently.

She glanced at me for a moment and without cracking a whiff of a smile said, "Ok" and returned her gaze to the mama-san who nodded in agreement.

"I will go get dressed. Wait for me?"

To which my drunken ass replied, "Better hurry or else I'm gonna disappear on you!"

She finally exposed a bit of a smile and departed toward the back.

"Let me buy you another beer," said the mama-san who also departed. Very soon I was sitting alone in the booth inebriated and jet lagged with two more beers and waiting for the most beautiful girl that I was ever about to sleep with.

I couldn't help but feel awkward. As I sat there fighting sleep with every breath, I began to experience an overwhelming feeling of inadequacy. I felt like a fool for being run out on. I was uncomfortably drunk and tired, and I believed this highly desirable girl would expect to be treated to a luxurious night out. Along with those thoughts, if I was taking this girl into my bed, I wanted to be able to perform. The anxiety I was feeling was likely to make my performance sub-par. I'd also probably have to deal with a conceited bargirl who would not make any effort to relax or arouse me.

I certainly had plenty of time to brood over these thoughts. By the time she reappeared from the back, my two beers were dry and I could only prop my head up with my hand. It was almost 1am and I had passed out before 9pm on each of my previous nights, though the site of Marian out of her dance clothes fired a bit of adrenaline.

Marian certainly knew how to look beautiful. She was wearing a long white evening dress with a jewel-studded white bolero jacket. Her clothes were not the typical cheap bargirl clothing. They looked like name brand apparel from an international clothing chain. A trained eye may have been able to pick the brand. She had removed most of her makeup leaving tasteful eye shadow, red lipstick, and blush that showed off her fair skin. Her dress, skin, and makeup all contrasted to her long jet-black hair to create a dazzling sight.

"You know I will be passing out very soon? I don't believe I can take you to High Society tonight," I said.

"It's ok. So, you want to go to the hotel?" asked Marian.

"Yes, I'll be lucky to make it even that far."

And with that, a goddess elegantly glided out of the bar towards Central Park with a drunken buffoon staggering beside her.

Marian entered the room and relaxed herself in the chair opposite the bed and seemed to just wait there. It was beginning already to look like the customer and beautiful bargirl experience I was expecting. *At least she wasn't on her phone.*

"Are you ok?" she asked.

"I'm exhausted," I said and crashed down on the bed fully clothed.

"Why did Star run out on me?" I asked lacking any better conversation.

"I don't know. She's my friend, but I don't hang out

with her much outside the bar. I think maybe she went to see her sister," Marian answered. "It's ok, it worked out for me."

"I'm surprised you were still there. It seems like you would get barfined much earlier in the night."

"Oh, why do you think that?" she asked.

To which I gave the obvious answer. "Because you are so beautiful."

She let out a shameless smile. It is something she's heard countless times I'm sure.

"So where are you from?" I asked.

"I'm from here."

"Here? As in, you were born in Angeles City?"

"Yes. My mother was a bargirl, and my father was Japanese," she answered. Of all the answers I could have heard that made the most sense, that was it.

"Did you know your father?"

"No, but I heard he was quite handsome!" she said giggling. In this instant, my sheer admiration for Marian turned to minor sympathy.

"My mother, she got drunk one night and didn't use a condom," she continued while still laughing.

"And she stayed in Angeles City after?"

"Yes of course. She worked in the bar a long time. When I was a kid, I would come to the bar. But she always protect me, everyone was nice to me. I liked the bar and always wanted to work in one."

A half-Japanese and half-Filipino bargirl was a treat I never had. After a half hour more of pleasant conversation, she finally offered, "Would you like me to come there?"

She stood up from the chair with the grace of a ballerina and I immediately became aroused.

"Take off?" she asked motioning to her dress.

I laughed and nodded my head.

She stood before me and lifted her white dress over her head to reveal her pristine fair skinned body with perfect sized breast and hips barely covered by white satin panties. Then she slipped under the covers next to me and laid her head back on the pillow and true to her form when she entered the room began to simply wait.

Flabbergasted and frankly, afraid, of the beauty next to me, I didn't move. I continued to lay on the bed staring at her.

"Are you ok?" she asked.

"I'm fine, how are you?" I asked sarcastically.

These are the kinds of encounters with bargirls that I loathe. I hate feeling that I will have to nearly rape them in order to fuck them. I began to paw at her tits and her hips. When I slid my hand under her panties to her clit, she asked, "Do you want me to take them off?"

I meekly answered "Yes."

She continued to simply lay there on her back waiting for me and I was quickly becoming annoyed and tired of the situation. I finally removed my clothes and began to prop myself above her when she smiled and coyly took the pillow and covered her face.

With that I took one final look at her immaculate body and collapsed on the bed beside her. Whatever was going to happen was going to have to wait. As I began to drift away, I heard one final question.

"Are you ok?"

That night I slept later than I had yet on the trip and awoke thankfully to find Marian sleeping soundly next to me. At least she did not share Star's behavior of running out on a paying customer, something she could easily have done and claimed I had every chance to get my money's worth. I dragged myself out of the bed and got in the shower to wash off the night's drunken bender. I could smell the alcohol in my breath and sweat.

In the shower, I decided I'd better make something happen soon. Besides, though this girl was beautiful, I couldn't be less interested in her conceited mannerisms. I was ready to be rid of her and go on with my vacation. When I returned from the bathroom with the towel around my waste, I saw that she was stirring.

"Are you ok?" I asked her smiling.

"Yes. I sleep well. You went to sleep so early."

I dropped my towel to the floor and climbed under the covers with her. She wiped her eyes and yawned throwing her arms out wide. Even with the smudged makeup and morning eyes, she still looked amazing.

I turned my body toward her and placed a hand on her stomach. As she started to lower her arm nearest to me, I gently guided it toward my crotch to which she showed no objection. She placed her hand on my rapidly hardening cock and slowly massaged with her fingers. I had made sure to block her access to any of the pillows on the bed, but instead she turned her head away from me. I decided at this point, she was not going to be the one to lay there while I climbed on.

"I want you to drive[17]." I told her.

"Ok, if you want," she said without argument. Up to that point, I would have thought any kind of service was to be out of the question, but I guess she was merely going to wait until I commanded her.

She reached over to her purse to grab a condom and then turned to face me. After opening the condom with her teeth, she grabbed my dick with one hand and then rolled on the condom like the professional she was. I had a raging boner at this point. I guess it's much nicer for beautiful bargirls. If she had been less beautiful, I doubt I would have been aroused so easily.

---

[17] Drive – Philippine sexual expression meaning girl is on top.

After I was wrapped, she rolled back over and produced a small tube of lubricant. She squeezed a peanut sized amount to her fingers and dipped them below and into her pussy, all the while holding a very stoic face.

"Ok, are you ready for me?" she asked attempting a smile.

"Jump on."

With that she placed her arm on my shoulder and rolled her hips on top of me as I rolled onto my back. She used her hand to guide my cock inside of her and then placed both her hands on my chest to gain leverage. Her jerking motions to bob herself up and down were borderline irritating, but like so many things with her, I ignored because I was busy fixating on the beautiful image that was straddling me.

As she repositioned her hands to the bed beside my shoulders exposing her armpits, I even caught a whiff of day old bargirl body odor, and I lamented that she actually WAS human! She was not a goddess, she was just like every other girl from Angeles City that I had had in my bed.

The sex however, could not have been duller. I may have been having just as much fun jerking off while watching her lie in the bed. "Ok, doggy style," I said. To which I thought I caught a glimpse of an "about time" attitude. Yes, don't worry dear, this wasn't going to last long.

When she propped her ass up in the air, I again was amazed at the site. A perfect ass, with perfect beautiful asshole, on top of a perfect cunt. I doubt even in all the porn I'd seen, there had been such a view.

I stabbed into it. Then, I grabbed both her hips and thrust in with as much force as I could muster. She hardly made a sound beyond releasing some air. As I thrust harder and harder, she even propped up her chin with her elbow. This was common for her. It was just a day at work and she was daydreaming in the same way I might be at my boring desk job.

I kept thrusting and pulling her skinny body into me trying to make it last as long as possible, but I was finished in the few minutes that I expected. I did not bother saying anything to her or trying to cuddle, I just went into the bathroom and removed the condom. When I came back in, she was sitting up in the bed still naked with a bit of a smile on her face. "Are you ok?" she asked.

I laughed. "I'm great dear, how are you?"

"I'm fine."

"Are you ready to go?" I asked her.

"Yes."

And with that, we both got dressed, as I was planning to head up to the roof for some coffee and breakfast.

"Will you walk me out?" she asked.

I smiled at the innocent request. She did not want to do the walk of shame to the front desk to have them phone my room, even though I'm sure she'd done the walk hundreds of times. I'm certainly not a man that would ever reject that plea from a girl. I accompanied her down the elevator and out the front door.

As I returned to the elevator, a skinny girl in a stylish blue dress with wonderfully thick wavy black hair walked ahead of me and pressed the button. As we stood there waiting for the elevator, she turned toward me and caught my gaze.

"Nathan?" she said in a look of surprise.

"Oh, hi Lynn!"

Lynn looked better than she had on my previous trip, though that could simply be the clothes she was wearing and her daytime makeup.

Unlike Ashley, who I had planned to see again, I did not have the same desire for Lynn. Since I never post my travels to Facebook, she had no idea I was there and it would have stayed that way had I not bumped into her.

She was heading up to see a regular customer, and I still did not intend to see her again, even though I was sure she'd now message me over Facebook at some point.

CHAPTER 9

My Favorite Door Girl

John and Allen ended up being my steady mates for a few nights. I alternated on nights between living it up with John and playing the cheap Charlie with Allen. I'd been in Angeles City for a little over a week of my three-week vacation and my jet lag was finally wearing off. I tried to keep a lot of variety in my day, but it usually started out at the Central Park roof eating the Filipino breakfast with a pot of coffee, then showering and getting a $7 massage.

The massage parlors in Angeles City are numerous and for the ones with no extra services, their quality usually runs about the same. They all have at least a little training in massage but none of them would rival a high-priced spa in the States. However, Jim showed me a massage a little off Fields Avenue called the Body Bliss Massage that had girls as well trained as any in the States. Still for the price 300 pesos, it is the best bargain on anything in the Philippines when compared to the prices you'd pay in Western Countries.

After my massages, I might pick up a girl for an afternoon play session... max 30 minutes. She would be a girl to tide me over, just a hole to stick my dick in. The bars around the Body Bliss Massage were pretty good for opening early and having decent talent. From there all the way down to Pony Tails, there was always a cutie on offer. And naturally, they are more than happy to take only a short time.

Afterward, I would try to accomplish some sort of work in my room if I felt like it and then head down to Tequila Reef to meet the wingmen. The night at Tequila

Reef would start the same every night. We eat some high priced but delicious food, John would get nearly wasted, I would get tipsy, and Allen would play nursemaid. Then we would head out and straight into one of the nearby Walking Street clubs.

"Not tonight man," said Allen as John was making a beeline for Crystal Palace again. "I'm tired of playing nice with these money-grubbing whores on Walking Street. Let's head down to Perimeter."

The idea sounded great to me and John was quickly persuaded as well. So, we turned left and walked down the back road past the entrance to Crystal Palace and Tropix and rounded the corner until we reached Fields Avenue and began to cruise away from Walking Street.

Bam! A stiletto boot to the groin is exactly how I would get customers into my bar! The door girl for one of the first bars you pass on Perimeter is practically an Angeles City legend. I've seen her every trip since I first came and her M-O is the same every time... stick her foot into the crotch of the passing potential customer. John loved it, he grabbed her leg with one arm and the rest of her with the other and carried her into the bar. She laughed hysterically and wrapped her arms around his neck. I could tell they knew each other well.

"Why you not come see me anymore?" she said to John. We had all sat down at one of the bar's high tables and she came to rest in John's lap. She was a nice-looking woman, a little on the older side for a door girl but what she lacked in age, she more than made up for in personality.

"I'm getting married!"

"Oh you bola bola[18]! If you marry, you marry me!" she said.

"Ok, I will marry both of you!"

---

[18] Bola bola – "You are bullshitting me."

As John and the door girl continued their flirting, I looked around at the bar. It was an older run-down bar and there did not seem to be many girls. There were customers though, and lots of them. Almost every chair was full. Either she is a very successful door girl, or …

"Hey you! Where are you going? I'll be right back honey," she said to John and went chasing after a group of guys heading toward the door. Ok, she must be a very successful door girl. I seemed to be immune to her charms on all my previous trips. I think it had something to do with being kicked in the dick. She never did come "right back honey," by the way.

We were about halfway through our first beer when a tiny girl appeared at our table. If I had seen her on the street, I would have assumed she was 14 or 15. I hoped that wasn't the case. If her body appeared mature to me, I would have called it attractive; skinny, very little tits, but attractive nonetheless.

"Well, how are you, little spinner?" Allen asked smiling like a pedophile.

"I'm good, will you buy me a drink?" she hustled.

"Will you spin around on my dick later?" Allen asked. This was the first time I'd heard him talk in this manner to a girl. He was usually more reserved.

"NO! I'm cherry girl!" she replied quickly.

"Yes, that's what I figured," said Allen.

"Drink! Please honey!"

Not the one to let a young girl go unsatisfied, John jumped in to buy the little girl a drink. I felt like a cradle robber as she jumped up on the empty bar stool between John and I and placed a hand on my thigh.

"How old are you? 14?" asked Allen.

"NO! I'm 18!"

"Sure, you are, let me see your ID," said Allen.

The girl just giggled and did not offer up an ID. It appeared to be missing from her outfit. Another girl I'd found without an ID, though I'd bet any amount this one was definitely not 18. She was put to work by someone to hustle drinks in the bar.

"How much for your cherry?" asked Allen.

"No! Only drinks, sir!"

"Well, how boring are you, little girl?" Allen mused.

After 15 minutes of Allen teasing the little girl, we decided to head on to the next bar. There just wasn't anything to see, unless we were trying to make friends with other perverts. As we walked out the door, I was spared from the boot in the crotch trying to keep us from leaving... John got it squarely. I think he liked it, and would have even gone back inside had we not urged him on down the street.

"So Allen, have you ever barfined a cherry girl?" I asked.

"Yes."

"So you took a bargirl's virginity?"

Without any shame, Allen answered, "Yes, and it was the first virginity I ever took. I was 50."

"How was it?" I asked him, in shock. Not so much in shock that he would take a cherry girl, more so that he would spend the money necessary to take a cherry girl.

Allen shook his head. "I wouldn't do it again."

"So, how much did you p---"

"HONEY! I'VE MISSED YOU!" a door girl yelled as she threw her arms around my waist and looked me in the eye from the level of my chest. I looked down to see the beaming smile, highlighted hair, fair skin, and black dress of the door girl I barfined earlier on the trip. I was smitten all over again.

And it certainly seemed like we were stopping in at her bar, as I was powerless to keep her from pushing me straight through the door. Just as before, she could have taken me anywhere. John and Allen followed. It seemed John had made a friend of his own from the door girls.

We found ourselves sitting at a booth in the bar of the door girl I barfined early in my trip. That night, there seemed to be better looking dancers available, and the western managers were still hovering around a back table. John had the other door girl sitting on his lap and my girl was sitting with her legs across mine and her dress pulled up so her fair-skinned tiny legs were exposed for me.

"What is this? Cherry girl night?" asked Allen smirking.

"How you know?" replied the little girl in John's lap. She looked young though not so young that she'd be obviously underage. Since she was a little chubby, it would not surprise anyone that she had managed to make it to 18 or 19 without much attention from boys. She had a wide face and short black hair matching the same black dress my girl had on.

"Well, this girl is not a cherry girl. In fact, she seemed to know quite well what she was doing," I said.

WHAP! Maybe I deserved that hard slap in the shoulder. Though she didn't actually seem to mind as it was accompanied with an overt 'I like the attention' laugh.

"Hey, what's your name anyway?" I asked her.

"What? You don't remember my name?" she gave me the standard reply.

"You never told me."

"Yes, I did!"

As I have had this conversation many times, I kept up with the standard line. "So, do you remember my name?"

"Michael," she said quickly.

Allen and I both laughed.

Her eyes opened wide in embarrassment and she giggled and started bouncing in the booth as she announced her second guess.

"Jim."

"No."

"Rick."

"No."

"Veika?"

"What the hell kind of name is that? Bet you don't know where I'm from either!" I said.

"AMERICA!" she announced proudly, smiled and tilted her head into my shoulder lovingly.

"I'm Nathan. Nay-than."

"Nay- tan."

"Nay- THan." I got her there eventually, I've gotten very good at it.

"I'm Jenny. Nice to meet you Nay-THAN!" she said and bounced up with a bundle of energy, gave me a big kiss, and then threw her arms around my neck and squeezed tightly for a good ten seconds.

I smiled and thought for a moment that I had just met the love of my life. There seemed to be an aura radiating from her that grew more powerful with each delightful little bounce. Butterflies in my stomach began to grow with each passing second, and I knew she was going to be mine for that night and possibly much longer.

"High Sol! High Sol! High Sol!" Jenny and her friend were chanting in our booth after drinking for an hour or so. I had barfined Jenny shortly after arriving in the bar. For the next hour, she attempted to talk John into barfining her cherry-girl friend. John didn't want to because he wasn't allowed to barfine, and wasn't sure if there would be a loop hole for cherry girls. Allen didn't want to barfine her because it was a waste of money.

Don't put bargirls ahead of your friends.

So, I barfined her, and agreed to bar-hopping only.

That is something I'd never done and vowed to never do, but at that point, I was wanting to make Jenny happy. What can I say? I was love struck.

John laughed with me and congratulated me. Allen practically ridiculed me.

"So, you want to boom boom?" I asked the cherry girl jokingly.

"Yes!"

The two girls laughed.

"She wants 100,000 pesos," Jenny said to me.

To this, Allen's beer went spurting out of his mouth. "You're joking!"

The girls' amusement turned quickly to frowns.

"Hey, she's nice girl!" said Jenny in defense of her friend.

"Good luck finding it!" said Allen. I wasn't sure at that point what his motivations were as he said earlier he would never take a cherry girl again. I guess it was probably the cheap-skate mind blowing a gasket at what he considered a high price for a chubby girl's virginity. In any event, I wanted to shift the mood back to the party it was a moment ago.

"You guys going to find some girls and come to High Society or am I going by myself?" I said to them.

"Fuck it, let's go. I can find a cheap girl at High Society. None of this 3,000 or ... 100,000 girls who think they are special," for the first-time Allen was irritating me. Though it was probably because I had fallen so hard for this girl, who was just a bargirl. There is a lesson here, don't put bargirls ahead of your friends.

Though, it did make me wonder how much he got away with paying for his cherry girl several years ago. I never did find out.

High Society is a well laid out dance club in the heart of Walking Street. In the form of similar dance clubs in Bangkok and Pattaya, it serves both the purpose of hanging out with friends or a girlfriend, and as a place to find freelance hookers. Any single girl in the club is looking for a customer and most girls as part of a group would also be available to the right customer.

The club itself wouldn't seem out of place in an American city, but if the five of us walked into an American club, you know, 3 older white guys with their 20-30 year younger brown girlfriends, we'd feel uncomfortable from all the stares. In High Society though, we were just one of the crowd. Most male patrons there had their young sexy bargirls with them trying to act out the joys of their youth. It is nice to prove to myself that I'm still that young stud inside, even though my body is moving on.

And no dress code. Well, how can you have a dress code in the Philippines? Jenny was wearing the same short jean shorts and yellow cotton shirt with flat shoes and I was in sneakers, jeans, and a white t-shirt. She was an awful dancer too, but in the cute way that no one would laugh at. I did my awesome feet planted waist shifting old white guy dance that I'm sure even there I stood out as ridiculous. Allen was scouting, and John was taking care of the cherry girl, trying not to touch. John seemed to be quite the dancer no doubt coming from years of experience.

After only 30 minutes, I was soaked in sweat. Jenny kept playfully wiping it away from my face. She truly seemed happy with me no matter what. I hoped it wasn't faked or just an "I'm happy because I'm getting paid" reaction. I know deep inside that's wishful thinking. These girls would not be interested in me if not for my money, but it is hard to convince my heart of that. Sometimes, I really hate when my heart gets away from me. It makes it even harder knowing they themselves may not understand that their emotions are manipulated by the wealth disparity between our culture and theirs.

Finally, I removed myself from the dance floor. I was worried they'd need to bring out a mop. Jenny and I snagged a small table off the dance floor. On cue, Allen showed up with a very attractive but seemingly battle-scared freelancer.

"One thousand pesos," he whispered in my ear. Yes, for that girl, it seemed like a great deal. I hope she didn't expect a tip, she probably wouldn't get one. My night was pushing 10,000 pesos so far, and in my mind, was worth every bit. He seemed triumphant in his acquisition, and headed out of the club.

I spent the next few minutes making out with Jenny, until John and his new girlfriend arrived at the table. And I thought I was sweaty! John looked like he had fallen in a pool. It didn't seem to bother the chubby cherry girl though. She was all over him. I've seen career hookers going for a mark that weren't so friendly in public.

"Hey hey, you leave my friend alone!" said Jenny, slapping John on the arm.

"Is this another loophole?" I asked.

He just shrugged his shoulders and returned the smooching. His hand was on a chubby tit and trying to pull her shirt down a little for a bare skin feel. She didn't even seem to mind. To me, it was a disgusting site. Cherry girl or not, I'm just not into fatty bargirls. John even had a beautiful wife! It's just the kind of thing that happens in Angeles City, you get crazy. In his mind, he was thinking he could pop this girl's cherry for free.

"You know, I'm the one who barfined her!" I yelled at them jokingly.

"Yea, thanks buddy!" said John coming up for a bit of air.

At first, Jenny had seemed a little irritated at the scene the two were making, but she quickly relaxed and turned her attention back to me. Cherry girl though she might be, she worked in a bar and needed no protection. I decided I should get Jenny out of the club anyway. If John was going to pop a cherry, it would likely be easier if the friend was gone.

"You hungry? I'm hungry," I said to her.

"Jollibee!" she screamed and erupted in happiness. I love how Angeles City girls are so easy. This would be like finding a beautiful date in America and her screaming "McDonalds!"

And so, a sweaty middle-aged western man left the dance club holding a lively bouncing young girl under his arm. Her energy was ceaseless. As we strolled down Walking Street taking in the late night drunk scene, she continued to sway to the music of High Society with a smile that read there was no better place in the world for her than that moment. I longed for the days of a carefree youth such as that, though I'm certain I never had it. I believe it's a personality trait to maintain such joy at everyday interactions. I wanted to believe I had something to do with it, but I doubted that was the case.

As we walked, she tried to help me dry off by pulling on my shirt making it flap, giggling the whole time. She moved behind me during the process and then stopped and slapped my ass as hard as she could in the middle of the street. I jumped around instantly attempting to return the favor, and she again erupted in giggles and tried to run circles around me. Though I think she found me to be a little quicker than she expected, and I ended up chasing her all the way to Jollibee. The site must have seemed ridiculous to the multitudes of onlookers, a sweaty foreigner chasing a young giggly girl down the middle of the street trying fruitlessly to slap her little bubble butt. I was feeling younger, happier, and more carefree with each passing moment with Jenny.

I almost enjoyed my butt slap when we reached the crowded doors to the restaurant but instead got a hug around the waist. I thought what an ingenious way to avoid another slap from me, or maybe my infatuation was progressing so that I believed everything she did was either brilliant, loveable, or hilarious.

"How long are you going to be in Angeles?" she asked me after sitting down in the packed Jollibee.

I told her about two more weeks.

"I stay with you?" she said in her normal cheerful attitude.

As much as at that moment, I wanted to answer, "Yes, please! And let's go to El Nido[19]!" I hesitated. I was, after all, on a sex vacation, not a wife-finding mission. So instead, I just smiled, laughed, and said nothing. I decided to change the subject.

"How long have you been in Angeles?"

In the questioning that followed, I learned she had come to Angeles City at the behest of her older sister who had lived in Angeles for five years. Her sister had started out as a bargirl but now stayed home with her two children who she had with a customer. The customer was an older American gentleman who had bought her a house and sent her money every month while visiting as often as he could. Though for some reason, he was reluctant to marry her and bring her to the states. When I hear stories like this, I always assume it's a very wealthy man who doesn't want to risk losing half his fortune to a prostitute.

Jenny was enjoying being a door girl. She seemed to have avoided any bad experiences in the two months she had been working. She claimed to only leave with a customer once or twice a week. Though, a girl with her appearance and personality, probably got barfined as often

---

[19] A beautiful tourist destination on the island of Palawan. As Philippine destinations go, it is pricey.

as every day. I didn't argue though, she was just trying to make me feel special, which I appreciate. That's really what I'm paying her for.

"Until I find boyfriend!" she answered when I asked her how long she planned to stay.

"What kind of boyfriend are you looking for?" I asked.

"I want American boyfriend. I like forty to fifty, I don't like young guy. They are butterfly. I don't care about money, I just want him to love me and respect me."

It's funny that I landed squarely in her qualifications for country of origin and age. Perhaps she was too naïve yet to understand that age doesn't determine whether a man will be a butterfly, especially not among men that visit sex destinations.

"There are tons of those men around here, I'm surprised you haven't found one yet," I said seriously.

"Only playboys," she said with a rare frown.

Rather than attempt to dig into the encounters with men she had so far, I changed the topic to Philippine customs and Angeles City life. For the next hour, we laughed and got to know each other in Jollibee. It seemed as though we had met each other at the mall or other venue where paying for her company was not the reason she was with me. We were simply a man and a woman getting to know each other due to a spark we had had.

As we walked to my room at Central Park, I remembered that I had never seen her naked on our first encounter. I wondered if she was going to be as shy this time. It seemed that we had gotten much closer, and after the night we'd had, I didn't even feel like I was her customer.

"Oh, this room is much nicer," she said as she casually strolled into the room, grabbed the TV remote and sat on the bed.

I looked at her sitting on the end of the bed switching stations and decided there would be no more "get to know you" phase. I approached her, dropped to my knees in front of her, and leaned in for a kiss. She coyly leaned back, and smirked with one side of her mouth, signaling that she was going to play hard to get. I was prepared to call her bluff.

With a smug, but playful look, she leaned slowly forward, closed her eyes and lightly kissed my lips. She then leaned back, opened her eyes, and looked at me. In a moment, her face brightened, her lips turned to a cheerful smile, and she threw her arms around me and locked her lips to mine. I moved her back onto the bed, and began to lift her shirt and peel off her bra. Despite the lights being on in the room, she put up no resistance.

Shirt off, I found the same creamy skin of her face with perfect young breasts, which for her tiny body were quite large and fit right into the palms of my hands. Her nipples were small and perky, and she moaned pleasurably as I leaned down to suck on them. I quickly removed her shorts and panties and raised up to see my prize for the night. As I ran my eyes over her body, she lay there without shame.

Though skinny, her hips were slightly wide on her small frame creating a voluptuous look that any man would find sexy. Her shaved young pussy was opened slightly and looked inviting. I dived my face in, inserted my tongue and tasted her day-old juices.

"Ahh," she squealed, and leaned forward to peer down at me. She pulled up one leg so as to give me better access and caressed my hair with her hand all the while watching me intently.

Soon, I was finished moistening her up and started

110

removing my clothes. She leaned back on the pillow smiling, and fingering her clit seductively as she waited. Remembering our last encounter, I quickly reached into the drawer for a condom.

"Thank you, dear," she said. "I'm ready for you."

As I entered her, the diminutive figure of my new love became even more pronounced. My dick looked not too much smaller than her legs to either side. I could not take my eyes off the site, my dick thrusting in those small sexy hips with the skinny legs splayed out beside. When she reached up to pull me closer to her, I was nearly startled.

She caught my mouth with her tongue as I dropped to her and let her extend her tongue into my throat. She seemed as lost in the moment as I was, the passion was becoming overwhelming, and speaking of overwhelming, I didn't last long.

Rarely do I spoon bargirls during the night, but she felt so pure and perfect under my arm that I quickly passed out.

I must not have been asleep for more than 30 minutes when I was startled awake by a girl screaming in the next room. It was not a scream of pleasure, it was a scream of pain and fear followed by the sounds of crying. A few seconds after that, she screamed "Fuck you" at the top of her lungs.

A brief pause followed by more screams of, "No! Fuck you! No! No! No!" followed by whimpers and again "Fuck you mother fucker! No! No!"

I looked at Jenny who was also awake and she shared my immediate concern. I wasn't too sure if I should get involved. Perhaps it was just a sex game or maybe the girl wouldn't want any outside interference? I didn't hear any screams of "Get off me" or "let me go," and for that matter since she was able to scream so loud, there wasn't any slapping or choking going on.

As the screaming persisted, I decided it would be better to do something just in case it progressed to something worse, so I called the front desk, who answered they would send security right away. Half a minute passed with more screaming when the girl yelled, "No! Please! Don't fuck my ass! Fuck you! Fuck you!" I was sure these were not screams as part of some game. She was screaming out of fear, so I decided to do what I could while waiting for security.

I threw some shorts on and rushed out of the room, ignoring Jenny's plea to stay out of it. I banged on his door as hard as I could and yelled, "Hey, what the fuck is going on in there? I've called the police, they are on their way!" The screams stopped immediately and for a moment, I was afraid I had just interrupted a sex game and there would be an angry man and her willing bargirl answering the door. Well, in that case, I'd tell them to shut the hell up as we were trying to sleep. Though, the door was never answered, and I stood there feeling like an idiot as it was now whisper quiet in the room.

I was relieved when security showed up. I quickly told them what had happened, and they knocked on the door and yelled something in Tagalog followed by the English, "Please open up, or we will be coming in."

The door opened, and a fully dressed girl appeared and walked into the hall away from the door and spoke to the two security officers in Tagalog. She was obviously shaken with tears streaming out of her eyes over smudged makeup. One of the officers banged on the door and said, "Come out sir."

A skinny 30-year-old Asian man appeared who I guessed was Japanese. Well, if he had tried something when it was just me banging on the door, I might have

112

taken him and been the hero! He scowled at the girl who again erupted in screams of "Fuck you! Fuck you!" To that, he tried to communicate to the officers something about her having promised a certain service.

"Ok, let's talk about this downstairs, let's go sir!" one of the security officers said rather sternly. The two hotel officers seemed professional and highly experienced in the matter. I wondered how often it happened. Up until that night, I didn't think it was common in Angeles City or any sex destination for that matter. Perhaps I was naive.

Jenny finally showed up at the door and we stood together watching them walk toward the elevator with the Japanese guy trying to plead his case. I guess he felt that it was ok to force whatever he wanted from a bargirl if she changed her mind about doing something in the room, or more likely, there had been a miscommunication at the bar and his intentions were lost in translation. The girl was silent and was holding her face in her hands. I felt bad for her. I'd certainly heard stories of similar incidents, but had never seen one first hand. I wonder what it would have progressed to had I not intervened. Oh and by the way, she never even looked at me, much less offered any sort of gratitude.

Jenny and I quickly removed our clothes and retired back to the bed in the same spoon position. As with most Filipinas, she was quickly back to sleep while I lay there for an hour or two calming my mind. The gleam from the city lights peaked through the curtains and glistened on her highlighted hair, and I began to feel a sense that I needed to protect her from any possible future atrocity. I asked myself, if I knew for sure that after I left Angeles Jenny would be subjected to an episode like we just witnessed, would I be willing to do anything about it? Would I want to send her money every month so she wouldn't have to work, or even marry her? The answer would never be obvious to me, as it never can be in a hypothetical world. I finally passed out reassuring myself it was not my responsibility to save her.

The next morning, I woke up to find ourselves in much the same position as we slept, except her head had moved further away, and her ass was pointed into my crotch. I was instantly aroused. I leaned forward and began to kiss and massage her silky golden back until she stirred. With a moan and a pivot of her hip, I knew she would be ready for more.

I leaned forward to kiss her neck to which she moaned more and commenced grinding her ass into me, my hardening dick being stroked by her firm butt cheeks. I reached my hand around her leg and slipped a finger onto her pussy to find it already wet. I was ready for her now, but there was no condom in reach. The mood would seem to be spoiled if I got up to reach for the drawer. Instead, I let things continue their course.

As I was kissing her neck, caressing her pussy, and letting her grind on my dick, she kept moving her ass up bit by bit until finally my dick slipped between her legs and contacted her inviting pussy. At this same moment, she turned her head to face me and shoved her tongue in my mouth, moaning her pleasure. With my hand, I guided myself into her.

As I'd never felt her without a condom thus far, the excitement was breathtaking. Her tiny pussy wrapped my dick tightly and it slid with ease through her naturally lubricated slit. With each moan, her little body contracted, squeezing me deeper inside of her.

After a minute, I rolled her onto her back and repositioned myself on top of her and she grabbed my hips and pulled, urging a faster pace. Being the gentleman that

I am, I began to drill her as fast as I could. She screamed in pleasure as I worked myself to orgasm.

I could not pull out, it was impossible. As I began to cum, I dropped down and pushed my tongue into her mouth. In return, she wrapped me tightly with arms and legs and moaned in pleasure as my semen emptied into her.

When I lay down beside her to look into her eyes, I saw that same look of utter joy and satisfaction.

With Jenny that morning, I broke one of my habits for sex trips and took her to breakfast. I normally enjoy a reset and alone time while I have my coffee and eggs, as well as flirting with off-limits waitresses, but that morning I did not want Jenny to leave.

The Central Park restaurant was busy as usual with its clientele of Western and Asian sex tourists with their dates from the previous night. The waitresses who had gotten used to serving me in the morning were a little surprised to see me show up with one, and were not as receptive to me. This is common in sex destinations it seems. Although I'm obviously a sex tourist, they treat me as if I'm a regular person when I'm alone but the moment I show up with a working girl, I become scum. Jenny even got dirty looks and attitude which upset me thoroughly, and I returned the attitude.

Jenny on the other hand couldn't care less. She was her usual cheerful self, just happy to be alive it seemed and restless to have some fun. One look at her convinced me not to take it personally and instead enjoy my breakfast with a beautiful person.

"I wonder how your cherry-girl friend and John made out last night," I said.

"Oh my God!" screamed Jenny and brandished her phone. This was the first time I'd seen her use it since we left the club. I wouldn't have cared if she did, but it showed either her interest in me or her professionalism that she didn't.

"I have no messages from her," she said, and she proceeded to text her.

"It's ok, I'm sure John took good care of her. I could think of much worse men to pop her cherry with," I said jokingly.

"No! She didn't!" laughed Jenny picking up the knife and threatening me with it, as if the words I uttered during breakfast could change the events between John and her the previous night.

"That was my first time," she said.

My mouth dropped, and I felt the budding feeling of jealousy inside me. She seemed as though she was talking about her first sexual encounter. "What?" was all I could muster.

"Korean guy, I got drunk," she continued.

The feeling of wanting to beat the hell out of some unknown Korean guy out there in the world swelled in me as I got the story of an innocent Jenny working the door at the bar as a cherry girl. Like her friend, she was willing to sell herself for a large sum, but didn't actually want to lose her virginity that way. She would barfine with guys but would never go to their hotel.

One Korean guy however, who she felt some attraction towards barfined her three nights in a row gaining her trust and on the third night, she decided she wanted to give herself to him, after 10 beers of course. I felt some relief that she had made the decision and remembered it, but I had still expected her to have lost her virginity long before coming to Angeles to work as a door girl.

"How long ago?" I asked her.

116

"Two months."

Well, she had certainly gotten busy since then. For a while sitting at the table, some senseless emotions began to build in me. It might have been jealousy, but it was more likely some ridiculous egotistical reaction to discovering I was with a girl who had never had sex with anyone other than paying customers and despite that fact, I was developing real feelings for her.

"So, what happened to the Korean guy?" I asked.

"He went home, and I think he not like me anymore," she said without any notion of sadness.

It seemed to me that the way she popped her cherry was fine with her. For me, unexplainably, it was not. I resented her for it, and in my mind, she was no longer the beautiful person she was 30 minutes ago. I look back on it and mock myself. I was choosing to be with sex workers, and I lucked into the company of a perfect girl but managed to find a flaw in her directly related to her being a sex worker.

By the end of breakfast, I began to feel like I was ready to move on from her. Earlier, I may have described my feelings as love, but that is the nature of Angeles City. Or is it? Maybe it is the nature of the men who visit Angeles City.

CHAPTER 10

Three Lesbians and Me

I pondered my emotional rollercoaster with Jenny during my daily massage. I promised her I'd see her again that evening, but my feelings for her had changed just enough from our conversation at breakfast that I was now ambivalent. Part of me longed to hold her close all night, but another part of me said it was time to move on to one of the many other hot young girls ready to spread their legs for me. When I checked my phone after the massage, a temporary distraction presented itself.

**Don't engage in talk of payment voluntarily,
it's much easier to get a good deal after
your nut.**

It was Lynn via Messenger. I had expected this message since she saw me in the lobby of Central Park, and it came at the perfect time. An afternoon romp with her would produce no confusing emotions and would save me from a barhop to find a short time girl, which I didn't have the motivation for. "Hello, how are you?" was the text, but in Angeles bargirl talk, that meant, "I'm available, would you like to pay me for sex?" Why, yes, yes I would.

On the walk back to Central Park, I convinced her to come see me right away. There was no talk of payment, which always makes me a little uncomfortable with girls I don't know well enough to know the expectations in advance. When it happens, I tend to use the lowest barfine in the city as a base. Maybe if I liked her or she was especially good, I would give more. The lesson here for encounters arranged outside a bar is don't engage in talk of payment voluntarily, it's much easier to get a good deal after your nut.

Don't send money to sex workers after returning home.

As it turned out at the end of the trip, she was obviously not happy with the amount I gave her. When I was sitting on the bus heading back to Manila, she texted me a sob story about her child getting sick and urgently needed more money. This is the Filipino bargirl way of asking for more money. I didn't give it to her, though if she had asked for more money at any time during one of our escapades, I would happily have offered it. Once I leave a sex destination, I do not send money to girls, which brings us to another lesson I shouldn't have to say, don't send money to sex workers after returning home.

It was almost 5pm, at least 3 hours after the text, when I got the call from the front desk about a visitor. She took Filipino Time[20] to the extreme in my opinion and I realized my afternoon quickie turned into an evening out. Maybe that was her intention.

Lynn looked amazing when she finally showed at my door. Perhaps I was growing tired of sub-20-year-old girls, and Lynn's maturity gave my brain (and dick) a refreshing bit of variety. She was wearing a stylish blue sleeveless pantsuit which gave just a hint of her slightly tanned fair Filipino skin. A smile beamed across her charming face, and that same thick wavy black hair flowed from her head.

Seeing her at the door, I realized she had a diminutive figure much like Jenny's but with her maturity and after having two kids, the curves had straightened out a bit and

---

[20] Filipino Time – It is customary in the Philippines to arrive after a scheduled time, instead of before. It can actually be considered rude to arrive early or on time.

she appeared more like a sophisticated skinny lady, very appealing to the eye.

"Hi Nathan, it's good to see you," she said somewhat robotically, with a fake cheer. It seemed to me something she'd said many times and I doubted she remembered any details from our first encounter. It was fine, I enjoyed playing the little game.

"Hi Lynn, I'm so glad I ran into you," I said ushering her in. "Are you still working at the same bar?"

"I'm not working in bars anymore," she replied.

She sat on the bed and we chatted for a while. I discovered her life had changed drastically since I met her. Although her husband had tolerated her profession for almost a decade, he finally met a new girl and left Lynn. The separation was upsetting to her, but she spoke of it as though it was merely a fact of life for her profession.

He still helped with the children, and this allowed Lynn to spend more time with customers and play the bargirl girlfriend routine with rich foreigners. It sounded like she had a few "boyfriends" supporting her. She may have even considered me an opportunity to add another revenue stream to her portfolio. I began planning for an escape shortly after sex.

The sex was mechanical as it was with her on my previous trip, but unlike the last time, she didn't jump right up and head out the door. In fact, she laid next to me under my arm as if a girlfriend. I wanted to not like it, but her petite mature body was a turn on to me. Unlike the young girls I'd had so much on the trip, she felt more natural to me, though there was still 15 years of age difference between us.

"So how is your girlfriend?" I asked her.

She giggled. "Which one?"

"How many do you have?"

"Now? I don't have any. Girlfriends are too much trouble for me right now. I miss my last girl though," she replied with a puppy dog look.

"I suppose it's hard to find a girlfriend if you are not working at the bars," I said, eager to continue the conversation.

"Yes, very. Now all the girls try to steal my man," she laughed.

"It's ok, I won't let them steal me," I said.

"Yea sure," she replied. "If you want, we can find a girl for us tonight."

I paused at her suggestion as it came as a bit of a shock. Immediately, I realized what she meant – that we go barhopping and find another girl to bring to the hotel with us for a threesome. Images of Lynn going down on a young bargirl while I fucked her from behind popped into my head.

"Well, what do you think?" she asked breaking the silence of my daydream.

"How will we find a girl?" I asked her. I was new to this kind of thing. I'd never barhopped with a girl searching for another girl.

"You pick one that you like, and I'll ask her if she likes threesomes."

That seemed easy enough, and my trepidation about having Lynn around for a while melted into jubilance and an eagerness to get the night started.

Instead of my normal khaki shorts and tee-shirt, I pulled out my slacks and polo shirt. It seemed like a special night to me, and I wanted to match Lynn's refined look. As we walked down the dirty Raymond Street from Central Park heading to Walking Street, I couldn't help but feel awkward. I felt like a rich man with a she-devil partner heading into the poor desperate district looking for a young girl to corrupt for the sheer pleasure of it.

Don't show off as it will invite trouble.

The beggar kids seemed to notice me at least, as a group of them surrounded me with their hands out, far more than had ever approached me on any previous nights. Perhaps, they simply didn't recognize me out of my usual attire and the more well-dressed visitors were more likely to hand over change. As is my usual habit, I kept my hands close to my pockets as they leaned on my hips to keep any of the more industrious of the kids from reaching in. After several "Wala's!"[21] and reaching the proximity of Walking Street, they finally relented.

From all my visits to 3rd-world countries, I've never been robbed or accosted in any manner. Perhaps I'm just lucky but I also make it a point not to stand out any more than is unavoidable due to skin color. If I am not expected to dress any better than jean shorts and a white tee-shirt, that is exactly what I do. The lesson here is don't show off as it will invite trouble.

Fortunately, there was no trouble to be found, only good times. In spite of the normal drab being cheap summer clothes, Angeles City is no different from any night scene. The more yuppie you look, the more attention you will get.

We turned right down Walking Street, and Lynn waited for me to pick a bar. A short way from Kokomo's, I decided on the Equus bar for no particular reason. I had never been in that bar and figured to give it a shot. It was a medium sized single-story bar again very typical of Field's Avenue. There was a long stage in the middle with a large selection of girls wearing a plain white swimsuit uniform. Around the stage were booths and the back extended into

---

[21] Wala – Nothing or No.

an area with a pool table and more booths. We picked a booth in the back but still with a good view of the stage. After sitting down, I noticed a hallway behind our booth that connected to the bar next door named Arcadia. The locker room seemed to be down the hallway as well. Our booth was in a great spot for exploring the bar's selection.

"Do you see any girls you like?" I asked Lynn.

"You choose!" she said, as she leaned back on my shoulder and peered towards the stage.

"What about her?" I asked pointing to a random girl.

"She's ok."

"The one on the end is pretty cute, what do you think?" I asked again.

"Ehh, ok."

Lynn's enthusiasm for picking out a girl seemed elevated in the hotel room, but now it seemed as if she didn't care at all and was just there to earn a paycheck, or maybe she was simply bored with the bar scene after having lived it for so long and every girl I picked would be the same experience to her. I hoped the night would get more exciting and soon.

After a couple beers and a full rotation of the girls on stage, I finally decided on picking one. She looked about 19 years-old, with a voluptuous figure, an innocent face, and modest highlights. I asked the waitress to call her over. Arriving at the booth, she sat on the outside of me and the other side from Lynn, I was not even sure she knew Lynn was with me. I told the waitress to bring her a drink.

"Hi, I'm Marilyn," she said offering her hand.

Quickly, I made the standard bar small talk finding out she had been working for about a month and was from Leyte. I introduced Lynn to her as my girlfriend, and then I dropped the bomb on her.

"We are looking for a threesome, have you ever been with a couple?" I asked point blank.

The look on her face was priceless and I hope when on my deathbed, I can find some joy from the memories of that moment. Her eyes opened wide, her cheeks immediately blushed, and she showed the faintest of smiles before answering in a drawn out, "Ummmm..."

Lynn busted up laughing and began speaking to her in Tagalog, to which I responded by slapping her on the leg and demanding English.

"I just told her it would be fun, and you are a nice a guy," said Lynn giggling, and again she spoke to her in Tagalog. I decided to let it go.

As she talked and laughed with Lynn, Marilyn's cheeks puffed up as she tried to hold back the grin of an experimental high school girl who wasn't sure about going through with it. I deduced she had not actually been with a girl yet, but that she had thought about it. This made me a little uneasy as there was no guarantee she would be comfortable with things once in the hotel room. I had built the night up in my mind and wanted it to be perfect.

They completed their conversation over her drink which had arrived, and then Marilyn looked down at her knees in a shy manner but still with a grin.

"I guess I can do it," she said.

I looked at Lynn, who caught my gaze and then shrugged her shoulders in an unsure gesture. Not knowing what to do, I decided to simply wait and enjoy their company and perhaps I'd find my answer. I ordered everyone another drink and encouraged more conversation hoping Marilyn would open up and act excited, but she didn't. She seemed interested and willing but scared and shy.

I began to think it would be fun to watch a young girl have her first lesbian experience with an older seasoned pro, but I was worried that instead she would not enjoy it and it would make for an awkward encounter in the room. I told Lynn this and asked for her advice.

"Up to you!"

"No, tell me what you think, do you like her?" I demanded.

"Up to you! Maybe she is ok. Many other girls that will have done it before," she said finally.

I turned to Marilyn and told her that we were going to keep looking but we appreciated her company. She seemed disappointed and said "Ok, sorry," as she returned to the stage.

"Let's go next door," I told Lynn since I'd looked over all the girls available in the bar.

Arcadia was a far more comfortable and spacious club than Equus. Instead of a rectangle stage running the center, there was a long stage that snaked through the club. The room was larger with booths neatly spaced to provide a laid-back setting for the customers. I had the waitress show us to a booth in the middle with a nice view of the stage. As I walked around peering at the current dancers, my eyes were drawn to a skinny young girl with short hair and seemingly enormous firm breasts.

Instead of waiting for the waitress, I caught her eye as I passed and signaled for her to join us. She smiled and casually moved around the other dancers to exit the stage and join us as we arrived at the booth.

"Hi, I'm Trixxy," she said. Yes, I made up that name. I wish I'd gotten to know her a little more as she was sexy as hell. She had Jenny's body with bigger boobs.

"You are so beautiful!" I told her, hardly being able to contain my desire for her. "Do you like girls?"

Trixxy's eyes nearly popped out just like Marilyn's but in her case, it seemed more disgust than thrill. I could hear a laugh from Lynn that seemed to agree with my assessment.

Trixxy shook her head and emphatically said, "No, I don't like."

"Are you sure? I would tip you really well!" I was desperate.

She shook her head again. Lynn laughed and leaned back and began ignoring us. In her mind, there was nothing left to talk about. The idea of leaving Lynn behind and taking this girl even entered my head, but not for long, there are plenty of hot girls like her to be found if that's what I wanted to do on a later night.

While waiting for Trixxy to finish her drink, I asked her the usual questions. She was from Samar, a province near Leyte, and had been working in Angeles for 6 months. She seemed comfortable in the bar, though the idea of a threesome must not have been raised that much. Oh well. She claimed to not barfine very often, which could be true if she was very choosy. With her beauty, she could wait around for only the best customers. I wondered if I would fit in that group if I were alone.

Soon I sent her packing and leaned back with Lynn.

"It's so hard to find a girl!" I said already frustrated.

"Ask the waitress."

I beckoned the waitress over, who had been hanging around close by since we were one of few customers, and asked her which girls would be up for a threesome.

"I think you will like her," she said pointing to a dancer on stage in her late 20s and wearing a long evening dress. The girl on stage caught our eye and started smiling and I leaned back to ask Lynn what she thought.

"She's pretty."

She was pretty... in the face. In her mid-section, I could see the slightest indication of a fatty belly bottled up by the evening dress. I was certain she'd had a few kids and that's why she wore an evening dress when most of the girls were wearing a bra and jean shorts uniform.

126

"I don't know Lynn. I think once you get that dress off, it's not going to be all that pretty," I said.

"Ok, you are right," agreed Lynn.

The waitress was not more help, so we waited for the next group to come out on stage.

"A willing girl doesn't seem as easy to find as I would have thought," I said.

"Very easy! Don't worry!"

As the next group of girls came onto stage, I was getting nervous at the prospect of propositioning half a dozen girls before I had to settle on some ugly girl desperate to do anything for money, but fortunately my anguish was quickly alleviated. There were plenty of nice looking girls in the new group and shortly after they all got to their spots on stage, two of them began dancing together seductively while watching themselves in the mirror.

The one in front was a young sexy girl with tanned skin and short black hair. Her face was caked with makeup that said, "Please fuck me." She had a small figure but not too skinny with a nice round bubble butt and large tits spilling out the top of her bra. She was gyrating her hips against an older girl who sported a taller and more muscular figure. The older girl looked like a gymnast or even a lean body builder. She looked to be about 28 and had one hand on the stomach of the younger girl moving in sync with her. The older girl behind seemed more focused on the younger girl while the younger girl was focused on them both in the mirror. They were definitely a couple.

I watched them for a minute or two and began to get turned on. These girls were obviously lesbians and wouldn't have any problem with the party I was looking for. I looked at Lynn who read my thoughts and seemed excited about them as well.

I asked the waitress to go get them. She scampered up

127

to the stage and rudely broke up their little grind. The two girls did not look too thrilled about it either and had questions for her. The waitress pointed us out and it seemed as though they begrudgingly agreed to leave the stage and join us.

The older girl plopped down in our booth with the grace of a boxer ahead of the younger girl who slid in delicately. After they settled in, I took a better look at their faces. I could see more masculine features in the older girl, and if I had seen her in a lesbian bar, she would not have looked out of place, though still attractive. The younger girl seemed more feminine and desirable. She may have ended up in our booth had she been dancing alone on stage.

"Hey guys, I'm Jody and this is Athena," the older girl said to me offering her hand with a firm grasp.

"Hi Jody, I'm Nathan. And Athena, right? How are you?" I asked while taking the softer hand of Athena.

"So, do you two know each other?" I joked.

The mood quickly lightened up as I got their story. They both had worked in bars for a couple years and had met recently. Athena was 22 and Jody was 26. Athena was from nearby Tarlac and Jody was from Manila.

Jody seemed crazy about Athena, constantly grabbing her and rubbing her legs, and Athena seemed to like the attention but struck me as a young girl who liked to play with everyone instead of a lesbian mainly into girls. Jody was dyke through and through, even saying she didn't like being with men.

"Have you two barfined together before?" I asked.

At this point, Lynn jumped into the conversation, which was fine with me, I'm sure she could get to the details much better than I could. I leaned back and let them speak in Tagalog and relished the occasional glances and giggles in my direction. After a minute, Lynn even seemed flirty with them both and Athena began flirting back. Jody was friendly and laughing but did not make any motions of attraction toward Lynn. After a while I got the gist of their conversation.

"Ok, they will do it. But Jody will only give you a blowjob and play with Athena, nothing else. Everyone can play with Athena and you can fuck Athena. Oh, and they want to leave early," Lynn said matter-of-fact-ly, as my dick began to grow in my pants.

"Do you two barfine together a lot?" I asked.

"Only a few times," Athena answered, "But it's ok, we like it. You have to use condom ok?"

"That's fine."

"Don't worry, he is nice guy, he will use condom," answered Lynn.

I still am amazed that it must be clarified at sex destinations, and though I was getting a little spoiled in not using them so far, I still considered it the proper thing to do.

"Ok, let's do it!" I said and paid the two barfines.

The two girls left, and Lynn wrapped my neck and started kissing my ear as if aroused.

"Very good choice," she whispered.

"It seemed like an easy choice," I said. "Which one do you like more?"

"Jody is sexy, I want her, but she said she only wants to make out with her girlfriend."

This surprised me, as I was certain she would like the younger hotter Athena. Maybe Lynn leaned more to the lesbian side than she let on.

"Athena is nice though," she continued. "I hope she has a nice pussy."

I nearly creamed my pants on the spot.

When the two girls appeared from the back, they were wearing matching outfits of jean shorts and a red tank top. They even had the same white fake-Nike shoes on. Athena had reduced her makeup a touch and both had their hair pulled up. They looked amazing, and I was about to have them.

"Let's grab a bite to eat first, ok?" I asked them. They nodded in agreement and we left the bar and turned right toward the Highway.

I took up my spot between Lynn and Athena with Jody clutching Athena on the outside as we walked down the middle of Walking Street. It was quite busy with lots of activity from local Filipinos out for a good time, groups of guys, and the many sex tourists like me. I felt like a king as I received numerous smirks.

As we approached Gossip, an open bar on Walking Street, the bouncer noticed me as I had stopped by there occasionally on the trip to smoke Shisha, and ushered me to the front table where I could sit to watch the happenings on Walking Street. "Hey my man!" he said shaking my hand. I was generous with the tips there and was well rewarded for it with the best seats and constant vigilance on my drinks and Hookah. "I'll get your Shisha, you want the same, right?" he asked to which I nodded.

"Hello Mr. Nathan," said the waitress who was standing over the table as we sat down. I ordered a round of drinks for us. Lynn and the two girls were getting friendlier by the minute as they discussed their drinks and ended up with 3 Appletinis. I had my usual San Mig Lite. They only wanted rice and chicken fingers, the usual for Angeles bargirls. I decided to nibble on the chicken fingers as well, I didn't want to load myself down before the main event.

As we smoked, drank, and ate for the next 30 minutes, I began to judge the personalities of the three girls. They were all comfortable with the situation, as they all had worked as bargirls for years. Lynn had a bit more experience though and the two girls seemed to show respect towards her. Respect among bargirls? Perhaps Lynn simply demanded it with her personality. She seemed to enjoy every minute of the evening and rarely didn't have a smile on her face. Jody also showed a great deal of personality. She enjoyed herself between coughs on the Shisha. Athena was relaxed but not bubbly like the other two. There was a bit of smugness in her attitude, which I guess came from being young and beautiful and between three people who desired her.

"Shots!" I said. "One round, how about it?"

Lynn agreed immediately, but it took some convincing for Jody and Athena to agree. We settled on Vodka. After a toast, Lynn and I downed the shot immediately while Jody sipped hers until it was gone. Athena sat hers down and stared at it, while I urged her on. Finally, Jody spoke to her in Tagalog, the two laughed, and she gingerly sucked it out of the shot glass, followed by the cutest look of revulsion.

Those shots certainly livened up the night even more... and seemed to exclude me even more. Lynn was flirting with Jody and Athena as if she was the one who barfined them. I tried to extract some attention whenever possible but regardless, I enjoyed watching them befriend each other. I hoped it would translate into a better party in my hotel room. Hopefully, that party would include me.

No one wanted to drag out the drinking. For myself, I was ready to get the party going in the hotel room. I think Lynn was ready to get the party going as well, and of course, Jody and Athena were probably ready to get it over with and go home.

Making our way down Raymond Street, we were joined by a boisterous young muscular American man and his beautiful bargirl clutching a dozen roses walking towards Central Park. He and his date looked to be no more than 21. Highly inebriated, he was making every effort to draw attention to himself and was handily succeeding. His date seemed quite taken by him. I'm certain if I was acting in that way, I'd have a near mutiny on my hands. Oh, I do miss those days, though I had never heard of Angeles City when I was 21.

"Oh my God! Look at you! You have THREE!" he yelled at me.

"No no, they are hers," I told him implying Jody and Athena were for Lynn.

"What?" he said confused.

"These are for me!" Lynn announced grabbing the arms of Jody and Athena.

"Oh my God, dude, you are my idol!" he said to me, and I listened to the drunken ramblings of a recently-made sex tourist all the way into the elevator. I did enjoy it a little. As beautiful as his date was (more beautiful than any of mine), I do believe he was slightly jealous. It is ok kid, all you need is money. I'm sure you'd do better than me anywhere in the world except there.

You are the customer and am in no way required of anything.

As we arrived at my hotel room and the moment was getting closer and closer, I found myself developing a bit of nervousness. While sex with prostitutes had long stopped being a new thing, sex with a lesbian prostitute couple and another bisexual prostitute who seemed way hornier than myself was far and away a new experience. I may have felt a bit of inadequacy as well. I tried to remind myself of another rule that applies to so many different

132

circumstances. You are the customer and am in no way required of anything.

I quickly took a shower while the three girls continued their conversation in Tagalog they had been having ever since leaving the bar. Afterward, Jody and Athena took their turn in the shower leaving Lynn and I alone on the bed.

"I want to eat Jody's pussy," Lynn said bluntly. "She is lesbian though. Fucking Lesbian. They are weird like that, saving themselves."

"Shhhhh, the bathroom door isn't that thick!" I said chuckling. If the shower wasn't running, they would have heard that for sure.

"Why do you like Jody so much? She's pretty, but not anything like Athena," I asked her.

"I don't know," Lynn said breaking a smile. "I think because I can't have her. She's charming though, and sexy for a lesbian.

"How are you? Are you ready for all of us?" Lynn asked me.

"Oh I hope so, though I'm a little nervous," I answered truthfully.

"Don't be nervous! You are the boss! You tell them what you want!"

That was good advice. Not really advice I needed though. Being the dominant customer in bed has never been that comfortable for me. A girl like Ashley who wants to be dominated is not common and I didn't sense that with any of these girls. It would be best for me if one of them was the dominant. Lynn seemed capable, though I suspected she was going to take charge for her own good instead of mine.

Jody and Lynn appeared from the bathroom wearing only towels and smiling happily. There didn't seem to be any nervousness between the two of them.

Lynn jumped up and bounded into the bathroom to

take her shower.

There was a bit of an awkward silence with Jody and Athena looking at me while I was not really sure what to do. I wanted to rip the towels off and plunge my body in between them and just grab on, but I didn't. I just sat there like a total loser until they burst into laughter in unison.

"Do you want to watch us?" asked Jody still giggling a little.

"Uh huh, yes!"

With that, they turned their attention to each other and playfully leaned together to begin a long smooch. At first the kiss was mechanical, but Jody quickly began showing some hints of passion, grabbing Athena's head with both her hands caressing her hair. Athena grabbed Jody's towel at the tits and unraveled it, letting it drop to the bed revealing Jody's trim muscular body.

Athena leaned down to suck on Jody's tits as Jody helped the towel covering Athena's young tight voluptuous body fall to the bed. Then Jody laid back on the bed pulling Athena on top smashing their breasts together where Athena could shove her tongue down Jody's throat. The scene displaying before me did not seem rehearsed and I leaned back against the headboard with a stupid grin on my face and enjoyed the show.

I'm sure that ridiculous grin grew even bigger when Athena swung around and lowered her hips over Jody's face and buried her head between her legs. I'd seen many 69s in my life ...on the Internet, but there was something more exciting about this one, I knew that I'd be a part of it shortly.

"Ahhhhhh!" laughed Lynn emerging from the bathroom. "You started without me!"

Lynn was giddy like a school girl as she scampered over to the end of the bed above the two lovers.

"Why are you sitting over there looking all weird?" asked Lynn. "Get over here, you can play with them," she directed me as she caressed Athena's buttocks.

I laughed and made some dorky comment about the grin on my face as I crawled beside them and began pawing at Athena's back as if petting a cat. I still wasn't comfortable. Lynn was massaging Athena's butt and the edges of her pussy when I suddenly got the urge to dive my tongue into Athena. Though there was only one hole available, I didn't let that stop me.

Athena's yelp was muffled a bit by Jody's pussy when my tongue contacted her exposed asshole. She didn't expect it at all. She took a moment to lift her head and peer at my face buried in her butt before returning to her duties.

Lynn was laughing hysterically, "Wow, you never do for me!"

Jody seemed excited by the attention to her girlfriend and I could feel the intensity of her cunnilingus increase dramatically. After a minute or two, Athena began to hang on Jody's legs lost in the pleasure. Another few minutes passed and she started crawling off, I guess it was too much for her. Jody and I wiped our mouths and I assumed my previous position leaning on the headboard. Athena crawled beside me and tucked her head on my shoulder and as if on cue, Jody grabbed my cock and began giving me the blowjob she had limited herself to.

"Ok, my turn to play," said Lynn as she buried her head between Athena's legs. I'm not sure the poor girl was ready for more as her face scrunched up and her body tensed. I was lost in the moment and began flicking her nipples to which she seemed to recoil from even more.

When I finally noticed that Athena was not enjoying the situation all that much, an idea hit me. Jody's ass was perched slightly in the air next to Lynn and seemed like it was calling for attention.

"Lynn, go down on Jody, she needs it, and I think Athena wants to relax a little," I said trying to camouflage my real intentions of helping Lynn get what she wanted.

135

The immediate reaction from Jody was a shake of the head still with my dick in it. Lynn came up to look at Jody with a plea on her face, and a silence fell over the room and... my blowjob ceased.

"It's ok, give your girlfriend a break, I don't think she can take anymore," I said laughing. If it was going to happen for Lynn, that was when it would have to happen. The look on Jody's face portrayed that it wasn't an impossibility, when finally the necessary nudge came from Athena.

"It's ok, honey, I want to watch," said Athena. I sensed she didn't really care either way but merely wanted to give her pussy a little freedom.

"Ok," said Jody as she returned to her duties and spread her legs slightly lifting her ass.

"She has a nice pussy, Nate, you should try it," said Lynn referring to Athena and assuming a position at the end of the bed between Jody's legs. Lynn's own ass hung off the bed and looked like it needed a dick in it but I figured that would stop the party for Jody.

I'm not sure it could have been less interesting for Jody but for me, the scene was exhilarating. I wrapped my arms around Athena and enjoyed a great blowjob and the sight of Lynn's face buried in Jody's pussy from behind while Jody's face was bobbing furiously on my dick.

After I figured enough time had passed for Athena's sensitivity to relax, I began to lower myself to her legs waiting for any indication she was not ready for more oral attention. A small smile when I looked into her eyes from between her legs told me all I needed to know. I dove in. I was a bit twisted, and we were now using every inch of the bed, but we managed to engage in a full end to end oral encounter. I didn't think of it at the time, but we should have gotten Athena to close the loop... though those logistics seem like they would have been complicated.

Funny enough, it was Lynn that stopped the action by kissing up Jody's back and helping out with the blowjob. She tried to get some kisses from Jody at the same time but they were only returned half-heartedly and she lost interest. Finally, Jody resigned herself by lying next to me on the bed.

This seemed to be Athena's time to shine, as she repositioned herself on top of me, condom in hand, and began to lower her hips toward my cock which Lynn was still servicing.

"Hey, I'm not finished!" Lynn laughed.

After passing the condom to Lynn, she slipped it on and then got one last quick lick on Athena before helping her settle on me. Athena's face turned to an impression that said, "I know you are loving this," as she quickened the pace.

It would be difficult to recount the different positions we engaged in. I vigorously tried to prolong the encounter by trying new things before I was about to cum. After a while, Lynn grew tired of the charade and lay on her elbow watching. Jody would occasionally attempt to excite me by rubbing my balls or ass, but after a while I sensed a bit of impatience which dulled the mood for me.

"Ok! I will cum dog-style while you are eating Jody's pussy," I announced finally.

And that is how my 4some ended... a smiling Jody staring at the face of her girlfriend pulsating into her pussy by my dick pounding from behind with Lynn laying on her elbows laughing at the difficulty Athena was having at keeping her tongue in contact.

After it was over, the two began heading out the door and I tipped them nicely for the amazing experience. Ironically, probably the best session of sex in my career of being a sex tourist was followed by the most masochistic. Naturally, I had no idea of the excruciating experience I was about to endure.

I was on Cloud Nine as I walked Jody and Athena to the door grasping at the last bit of hugs and kisses for the tip that I could get before they left. When I returned to see Lynn lying on her back with her legs spread eagle and biting one finger with a big smile that screamed, "I hope you have more," I felt as if I owed her for the experience I just had. I felt that it was my duty to pleasure her in whatever way was necessary to show her my appreciation.

It never occurred to me that I would be trying to get off a career bargirl that has probably had every sexual experience possible, had been pleasured orally by the best lesbian bargirls countless times, and who didn't seem all that interested in men anyway. Of course, I didn't really have all that much choice. My stamina wasn't quite there, using my tongue was the only option.

The grin never left Lynn's face as I plowed between her legs face first. She certainly enjoyed it. After-all, she really didn't get that much attention during the foursome, she was horny as hell, and she started the instruction right away.

Being instructed on how to eat pussy is a big turn-on. Most girls just lay there acting like they enjoy it and maybe after a few sessions, I can learn how to hit their buttons, but it is not as exciting as a girl taking charge over her own pleasure. I just never could get it right with Lynn, however. She wanted it hard, but not too hard, and slower than any other girl. She wanted as much of my tongue in contact with her clit as possible but didn't like me to go too low.

I don't believe it was frustration so much as it was that she finally got me positioned the way she wanted when she put her hand on the back of my head and began to thrust her pelvis into my mouth. The result for her was obvious to me, she was putting pressure between my tongue and her clit, and way more than I could have applied myself.

At first, I was immensely excited. She was going to grind my face in order to bring herself to orgasm. I was starting to harden up again. I couldn't wait for her to cum so I could fuck her again.

The orgasm didn't come though and the thrusts began to get more violent. She was loving it. Her moans were increasing and she began to get lost in the euphoria, but the whole time, my tongue was being smashed into my bottom teeth and the pain was starting to grow. I tried to resituate my tongue and my head to relieve the pressure a bit but Lynn would quickly correct me with a look of "don't move now, I'm almost there!"

That cycle seemed to continue for an eternity. I began to deal with the situation in my mind the way someone might deal with an excruciating fitness routine. "Almost there." "Just a little more." "The pain isn't so bad, go to your happy place." "Think of all the reward." Though all that quickly reduced to, "Why the fuck am I going through this for a bargirl?" My hardening dick was also stopped dead in its tracks, there would be no hate fuck immediately after, but the one later on I was beginning to plan with meticulous detail.

The submissive aspect of the encounter would have been an immense thrill had the pain not grown so intense. Though it may not have taken as long as it seemed, when she finally climaxed with a muted squeal, I gratefully raised my head to see the satisfied look of Lynn and taste the blood in my mouth. And apparently, it was also visible.

"Oh my God! Honey, are you ok?" said Lynn covering her mouth.

My response to her included a "Jesus Fucking Christ"

139

as I scampered into the bathroom with her following behind chuckling.

As I was examining the underside of my tongue in the bathroom, Lynn couldn't have acted more entertained. She was carrying on like it was the greatest thing she'd ever done. I was actually a little upset with her, though I had no reason to be, I could have stopped it at any time. My anger gave way to desire quickly though as she fondled my soft dick and through giggles complimented me with statements such as, "You are so good to women" and "My hero!"

The hate fuck did eventually commence. Since I had been drained during the day with two great sessions of sex and had to concentrate on holding my tongue in a certain way to keep it from aching, I was able to fuck that girl until all she could do was lie face down in bed and take it.

CHAPTER 11

The Corruption of Marilyn

Lynn made for a fantastic girlfriend in the days following the encounter with Jody and Athena. In just a short time, we were adapting to each other the way a couple does. She enjoyed me because I would treat her to nice meals and other luxuries and I enjoyed her because there was not an ounce of jealousy towards other girls. Having such an open relationship, even if artificial and short-lived was a fun new experience for me. The days were spent lounging around and trying new places to eat in town before heading out to a bar crawl in search of a girl willing to come back to the hotel and fuck both of us. The expectations were set very high with Jody and Athena, however, and I never got close to matching it.

The first girl was picked up at a bar across the street from Kokomo's. She was beautiful, but it seems looking back on it that she simply wanted to get barfined as quickly as possible and leave shortly after. The fact that she was being picked up by a couple was almost irrelevant. She played a little with Lynn, but was not into it and therefore neither Lynn nor I was too interested in keeping her. We shipped her out the door as fast as she wanted, much to her pleasure.

This kind of barfine is all too common and I should have seen the telltale signs of it in the bar when we were picking her up. The big clue was feigned interest. When engaged, she acted like the happy bargirl telling us what we wanted to hear and acting excited, but when she was not engaged, she would peer off into the club and look bored.

The following night, we picked up a girl from Pony Tails after an exhausting bar hop. I made every effort to find a girl that was into other girls and would love to eat pussy as well as take dick. I did manage to find a girl that liked to eat pussy, in fact, Lynn and she had a marvelous time. When I became involved, it was half-hearted, and perhaps simply watching two girls make out had already lost its appeal. After I busted a nut with Lynn instead, I even retreated, feeling like a third-wheel, and let them have fun until the early morning.

And in case you are wondering, there was no more sadistic face grinding and if Lynn didn't find her satisfaction with the girl, she was on her own for that. Instead, we had deep conversations late at night that became very interesting, ranging from the other boyfriends she had currently to the different girlfriends she'd had over the years. Speaking with Lynn, I may even conclude that being a sex worker in Angeles City is a pretty cool job with lots of interesting people that come and go in life.

Having been married for most of her career, she usually focused on finding a customer as quickly as possible, doing the deed and going home. While she would keep in contact with some customers, staying out with them for an extended period was rare and usually meant bringing home a great deal of money that her husband would accept. Even so, it was often the customer that did not wish to engage with a bargirl that was married. After considering it, I wondered if her being married would have changed my mind concerning the few days I had spent with her. I told myself that it wouldn't. Why should it? But I couldn't help but think there would be something different about it if she were married. Could she truly be as enthusiastic about it if she had to go home to a family? Additionally, I'd expect payment to be a much touchier subject. So far, she'd been happy with the 2,000 pesos I was giving her every day.

Since splitting up with her husband, which she had been expecting for some time, she had proceeded to let loose, not only taking advantage of some money-making opportunities she'd had to hold back from, but also allowing herself to enjoy her encounters more... which she was doing immensely. She was able to accept the adoration from rich visitors in the forms of vacations to Palawan and Boracay as well as shopping excursions that outfitted her wardrobe.

Barhopping with a customer in order to find other girls to take to bed: That's what she was enjoying the most though. Playing with girls throughout her career had been allowed by her husband, even engaging in the occasional threesome with him, but there was something different to her about participating in the purchasing side of it, a taste of which was rare while she was married due to the nature of the time limits imposed on her work day. As an experienced woman now, it was exciting to give young girls that first experience of sleeping with another woman.

"Do you remember that girl from the Equus Club on the first night? What was her name? Marilyn?" I asked her late at night.

"Yes! She was very shy though, I'm really not sure if she would be up for licking pussy," Lynn responded.

"I say we give it a shot. Let's go there tomorrow night and get her drunk and see how comfortable with it she appears to be."

I was desperate to find a sexual encounter as interesting as Jody and Athena. The last two experienced girls were lacking excitement, so I thought it was worth seeing how far I could push a new girl.

The polo shirt and khakis of our first night out

together didn't last past that night. I was back to wearing a tee shirt, jean shorts, and flip flops. It really didn't matter anyway, beyond making me feel a little better about myself. Now I was very comfortable with Lynn and no longer felt the need to impress anyone. Lynn still looked ravishing though, to the extent that we just seemed weird together. Surely, she could find someone better than this bum to hang out with.

We headed towards Equus at around 8:00pm which is a good time to catch the bar with most of the girls who work at night still available. Entering the club, I noticed Marilyn on the stage, but instead of calling her down immediately, I elected to stroll in and have a seat at a booth in view of the stage. I thought it might intimidate her if we picked her out right away. Though I'm sure she saw us come in and walk past the stage, she did not acknowledge us. It's likely she thought we were not interested in her after our meeting a few days previously – a big surprise was coming her way.

"Are you going to call her over?" asked Lynn after we had our drinks and sat for several minutes.

"Yes, I just don't want her to think we came only for her," I answered.

"Oh pffffft!" responded Lynn. By now, we had advanced our relationship to a stage of being able to tease each other. Any time I engaged in some sort of game playing in a bar, Lynn would respond with ridicule.

"You better hurry, she is the prettiest one on stage and there are lots of customers."

I could not disagree with her logic. Marilyn did seem to be a few levels above any of the other girls on stage, though the overall level of talent in that bar was a bit lower than others such as the Acadia Club next door. Instead of asking the waitress to grab her, I strolled up to the stage until I was right in front of her so I could judge her reaction to seeing me. She didn't recoil at least, that was a good sign.

A somewhat confused blank look turned to a smile of appreciation when I motioned to her to come join us at our booth. I met her at the end of the stage to take her hand and lead her to the booth. Lynn, the good sport, had turned on her welcoming flirtatious personality as we both arrived.

"Do you remember us?" I asked.

"Yes of course," she answered. So far, she was showing no signs of being turned off. In fact, I was detecting a bit of excitement exuding from the young girl.

"Drink?" I asked her. Obviously, a silly question but it's how the beginning of the relationship was going to have to start. Her drink was some sort of watered-down alcoholic drink, but at least it wasn't dry. It was a good sign that getting her a little drunk was not going to be difficult.

Lynn had already started the full-on flirting in Tagalog that had become habit. The conversation was unmistakably about me, based on the constant turns to my direction and giggling. Marilyn's expression would turn from hysterics to bashful recoils as Lynn's personality brought to life whatever story she was telling.

"Whatever she is saying isn't true," I finally interjected.

"I'm just telling her about how much you have been talking about her today. All day! All I can hear about is Marilyn! Marilyn! Marilyn!" Lynn laughed.

"WHAT?!?" I was nearly in shock. My plan of not letting her know that we had come just for her was already blown up.

Marilyn's face was turning red as she looked away from me embarrassed. It should have been me that was embarrassed. I guess I had to roll with it.

"Well, you are just too cute!" I told her while slipping my arm around her shoulder.

She really was cute and she had adorable mannerisms, like the shy girl next door, but hopefully with a wild side.

"Have you been with a couple since the last time we saw you?" I asked her. I might as well get straight to it now since my plan of easing her into it seemed shot.

"No."

"Well, we would love to take you home tonight, but are you sure you are ready for it?" I asked.

"Ummm. I think so. I want to try," she said. It was the same excited but nervous attitude she had the first night we met.

"Ok, but I need to know you are ready. Kiss Lynn right now and I will barfine you," I said. That just popped into my head.

"Ahhhh! See how you are!" laughed Lynn slapping me on the leg. Now it was Lynn who was embarrassed.

Neither of them turned to each other immediately. I caught them both off guard, but now I was determined to either make it happen or send Marilyn on her way.

"It's ok girls... here," I said taking Marilyn's hands and putting them in Lynn's. Poor Marilyn's cheeks were puffed up bright red and though she sported a shy smile just could not bring herself to look in Lynn's direction. I knew Lynn was ready and would take charge if I could just get Marilyn turned toward her.

And then it happened. Marilyn turned her head and lifted her eyes to look at Lynn. After Lynn caught her gaze, she responded by smiling and bringing her hand up to her cheek in a playful manner. Though I'm not sure, when Marilyn's head went forward and contacted Lynn's lips, it seemed the final push came from Lynn's hand.

The kiss was sad. At least, it would have been if not for the situation. Butterflies were filling my belly. I'm sure they were fluttering madly in Marilyn's. Lynn's eyes were wide open and she was holding back chuckles while Marilyn's eyes were closed tightly. The kiss lasted about 30

146

seconds until Lynn stopped and said, "Ahh, she's so sweet," and placed her hands on Marilyn's shoulders to lean her body into hers in a loveable way.

I could detect nothing from Marilyn that would indicate she was going to grow cold later. In fact, it was the opposite. I sensed she was excited not only to be barfined but by the sexual encounter she was bound to have. Excitement was building in me as well. It was a new feeling that I was having, a predatory instinct. I wanted to corrupt this girl. I wanted to push whatever boundaries she may have. She was becoming merely an object in my mind, a toy to be played with and thrown away.

As we waited for Marilyn to get dressed, I wrestled with the decision whether to take her to Gossip or to take her straight to the hotel. The upside to Gossip was the opportunity to get drinks in her and possibly loosen her up more, but it seemed she was already willing and perhaps there would be no better time. I decided to just go straight to the hotel, partially out of believing she would be eager to get dirty regardless, but I was mainly just impatient.

She emerged from the dressing room wearing a long white shoulder-less dress with blue flowers. I see some of the girls wear these types of dresses in the Philippines, it seems to be a fashion trend. To an American, they look like something that might have been worn in the 1920's by a conservative southerner, and likewise, it seems that only the more conservative girls wear these types of dresses. Of course, I'm no fashion expert and perhaps the notion that a Philippine girl's dress would have anything to say about their personality is my own mind's total fabrication. But... I enjoyed the thought immensely. I couldn't wait to soil this conservative daddy's girl from some farm on Leyte here to make money for her family.

Lynn and I both stood up to meet her so we could take our leave of the bar. As I saw Marilyn standing beside Lynn, the age differences really struck me. Marilyn was ten years younger than Lynn and while that isn't much between a man and his sex worker, it is an eternity among the sex workers themselves. Marilyn wasn't even in her prime yet, she was still in the nervous inexperienced domain when she will be chosen purely off her youth. Lynn was past her prime, she was now in the domain where she had to hustle for money by convincing her customers she was worth every penny. I didn't figure Marilyn would ever get to Lynn's domain, but I might change my mind after tonight.

"Let's get some drinks!" exclaimed Lynn, before I could tell her my desire to go straight the hotel.

Marilyn smiled and nodded her head in excited agreement, putting to rest any notion in my mind of going straight to the hotel. I couldn't be the stick in the mud that didn't want to party a little, but I was not about to let them camp out in High Society, who knows how long that would take. I informed them that we'd go to Gossip, to which they were fine with.

Bubbly with personality as she usually was, Lynn grabbed Marilyn's arm and escorted her out the bar with myself following closely behind. My excitement continued to escalate seeing the skinny elegant pant suit of Lynn alongside and directing the voluptuous conservative dress of Marilyn towards our date with debauchery. I begin to plan the sequence of events that would happen in the bedroom, hoping they could come to fruition.

The picture I formed in my head was of Lynn leaning back against the headboard in the room at Central Park with a small hole cut out in her pantsuit exposing her pussy to Marilyn who was leaned over on her knees still

148

wearing her flowered dress. I approached from behind and lifted her dress over her back exposing her soft young ass to me. Then I slid my dick gently into her asshole as she continued to dine on Lynn.

Of course, nothing is ever that easy when it comes to fucking a girl's ass, and I tried to snap myself out of it.

Exiting the bar and walking the short ways to Gossip, my attention veered off to the multitude of heads turning toward my dates. I love this feeling, even though I know it is utterly bogus. They are not mine and they could be any of these men's dates on any other night, but I have felt that momentary jealousy towards a sex tourist walking with his date or dates down the street, and I knew these guys were getting it over my dates, and that made me euphoric with pride.

"Hey my man! I have your table ready, right this way!" said the bouncer who was standing far out in the street and noticed me coming.

We ordered the usual Shisha, Appletinis, and rice and chicken fingers. Marilyn was eager to try the Shisha, though she coughed the same as all the girls and she began sucking down her drinks like she couldn't get enough of it. *An Angeles City bargirl in the making.*

"So have you really never been with another girl before? Even in school?" I asked her.

"No, never, I promise. Well, uhh, I did kiss my friend in 9th grade!" Marilyn answered to which Lynn and I busted up laughing.

"Tongue?" I asked.

"No! No, gross!"

"Gross? What's gross? I just saw you tongue kiss a girl!" I exclaimed.

"That's different. She's not my friend!" answered Marilyn giggling.

"Ok, I don't want to be your friend then," Lynn interjected while leaning towards Marilyn flirtatiously.

Marilyn returned a smirk in Lynn's direction that seemed to say, "I know what you want, and you can have it anytime."

While certainly reserved, Marilyn was more laid back than I expected her to be and she seemed fully engaged with the moment. She was not peering off to the street uninterested or looking at her phone, she seemed as though she was enjoying herself. I was happy with my pick, though I'm sure Lynn's incomparable ability to flirt and liven up the mood played no small part.

"She likes blowjobs," said Lynn turning to me after a lengthy Tagalog conversation and another drink had passed.

"Oh really?" I asked. "Hmm, what about eating pussy? You think you like that?"

Marilyn's eyes widened, and she began to cough madly on the Shisha as she answered, "Uhhh, I don't know!"

"It's ok, I will show you," I answered.

To that, Lynn chimed in, "Oh really? Are you going to eat me out again?"

"Fuck that!" I responded, to which Lynn laughed and Marilyn gave a puzzled look.

Lynn turned to her and started another lengthy conversation in Tagalog, at least lengthy for the event that I'm sure she was telling. Marilyn would look at me and smile at times and at other times looked plain frightened. I don't believe she had any desire to be face fucked the way I had endured.

"Oh don't worry!" Lynn laughed. "With man is ok! They are strong!"

By the late hour we left Gossip, I had achieved my

goal of getting a few drinks into Marilyn. She was at the perfect state of being drunk enough to lose any inhibitions she may have, but not so drunk that she might pass out or become oblivious. She was loose and the three of us strode down Walking Street toward the hotel laughing with each other. We had become as comfortable together as three people can become on one night.

At the hotel, none of us wanted to delay the main event any longer and Lynn and Marilyn both went into the bathroom for a shower. I was not invited. They were conversing in Tagalog, and I remained impressed at Lynn's ability to make Marilyn comfortable, especially considering that she was about to engage in bisexual sex for the first time in her life. Though, they didn't seem to be getting that started in the shower.

When they emerged from the bathroom, both wrapped in towels, Lynn motioned to me that it was my turn. Things seemed somber and relaxed as I entered the bathroom, they were sitting on the bed continuing to discuss things that I'd never be privy to.

As I stood under the shower, I realized the night was progressing much like the night when Lynn got all the action and I mostly laid around watching. I pictured myself laying on the bed while Marilyn ate Lynn's pussy all night, getting instructions. Lynn would say, "Hold your tongue right there. Ok, lick up and down a little on my clit." It was an exciting thought, but it just wasn't enough.

As the water ran over me, I stood there thinking I didn't want Lynn to monopolize the night again. When I got into bed, I'd take charge over Marilyn. I'd built some ideas in my head about this night and did not plan to let them slip away to a dominating lesbian. It might be the girl on girl experience that was new to her, but I bet I could educate her on a few things as well. I sped through soaping off and exited to find there to be no more towels.

I walked straight out of the bathroom naked and

dripping. "Hey! You couldn't leave me a towel?"

They giggled as I made my way for the bed. I hopped in between them on top of the sheets and gave them a great excuse to drop their towels. I laid there on my back watching Marilyn remove her towel to pat me down.

Her body was skinny and attractive but nothing particularly special for a Filipina. She had slightly large but a touch droopy breasts. Her hips were wide and her stomach was flat. She had brown skin on her arms which changed to a lighter shade on her chest and stomach. She wasn't shy at all, she removed her towel and modeled herself to me for a moment, to which I began to get hard.

Marilyn was wiping down my chest as I looked into her eyes, while Lynn patted down my legs and crotch. "Woh! Already?" she laughed as she gently patted down my dick.

Marilyn smiled and looked at my dick. Then she looked at me and licked her lips.

I reached my arm around to her back and leaned her forward to me. Dropping on top of the towel and my chest, I finally got my own kiss from Marilyn and it was far better than the one she gave Lynn in the bar. It was passionate and wet. Lynn laid down next to me, removed her towel from the bed and massaged my dick with her hand while watching intently our kiss.

Then she started giving me her own kisses on my neck, all the while massaging my dick, causing me to reach full erection. I noticed her kisses were coming closer and closer to Marilyn, she was wanting to steal my smooch, so I wrapped my other arm around her neck to control how far she could go. I was not finished.

In fact, I had a better idea and I began to nudge Lynn down toward my crotch. At first, she was obliging and seductively kissed down my chest, but as she approached my dick and was free of my arm, she skooched across me, draping her thick hair across my crotch, soaking up any water that was left, and began kissing Marilyn's hip, to which Marilyn's focus on our smooch was broken and she looked down at Lynn in a shy terrified way… *yes, there was a woman trying to lick your pussy dear.*

While a little perturbed not to be getting a blowjob, I became fascinated at what Marilyn's reaction would be. She was not in a position to easily spread her legs. She was sitting on her butt with her legs curled up towards my legs and her upper body leaning on my shoulder. Lynn was now kissing her top leg with a hand around behind massaging her butt.

Lynn caught her eyes as Marilyn turned away from me, then Lynn closed her eyes as she proceeded to delicately kiss toward Marilyn's knee. I reached out my free arm to caress her breast, and at this time, I could see some excitement coming to Marilyn's face. She was getting a great deal of attention.

"Relax dear," said Lynn looking up again as she reached Marilyn's knee. "Kiss Nathan some more, he really loves it."

With a shy giggle, Marilyn turned back to me and began a slow distracted kiss. She was obviously more interested with what Lynn was doing.

As soon as she wasn't looking, Lynn began to lift Marilyn's leg until her knee was pointed toward the ceiling. Her pussy was now exposed and Lynn began to kiss up the inner thigh of her leg. As she moved her body up, she slid across my dick as I continued to watch Marilyn's eyes.

They were wide open. She was still kissing me, but it was mechanical, she was far more attuned to the action below.

I knew precisely when Lynn's tongue contacted Marilyn's clit. Her eyes momentarily glared as wide as they could go and she let out a muffled moan and then could no longer keep her lips locked on mine.

We both looked to see only the bottom of Lynn's chin as her head was pushed between her legs. She was licking in slow passionate strokes while her arm was reached behind Marilyn's butt pulling her hips forward.

I held Marilyn, who was growing more excited, while I reached down to massage Lynn's ass and pussy, to which she responded by swaying her body against me. Marilyn's arms were curled up against me as she focused on Lynn's actions between her legs.

Lynn's arm made its way completely around Marilyn's hip to hold her pussy tight against her mouth and as she began to increase the speed of her licks, Marilyn began to make noises in enjoyment. As her excitement built, she began to roll her head back against me and drop her knee so she was more on her back and it seemed Lynn must be getting smothered.

Finally, Lynn came up for air and giggled in that charming way only Lynn could after eating pussy as she looked at the excited face of Marilyn, then she repositioned her body off me and barely clinging to the end of the bed, lowered her mouth again to Marilyn's pussy and gently licked her clit while watching Marilyn's reaction. I was losing any attention but for now, I was ok with it. Marilyn seemed to be thoroughly enjoying her first lesbian experience.

"How is it dear?" Lynn asked, lifting her head briefly.

"It's amazing!" Marilyn exclaimed moaning as Lynn's tongue again glided into her pussy.

Marilyn closed her eyes and began rolling her hips, getting lost in the moment. Still holding her head, I began to play with one breast as she massaged the other. She began to grow louder and moaning, "Oh my God!" she was no longer shy at all.

Marilyn got her pussy eaten for a good ten minutes, before Lynn came up saying, "How was that? You want Nathan to go?" *something which I had not offered at all...*

154

"Ummm," replied Marilyn bringing her finger to her mouth in a nervous expression.

"I want to do you," she said to Lynn. *Yes, much better idea!*

Lynn laughed loudly. "You want to lick my pussy?"

"Mhmm... I want to..." she repeated unable to hide the nervousness in her voice.

Lynn lifted to face Marilyn and brushed the hair out of her face. "You are so cute..." she said. Then she positioned herself between us.

"Oh my God, the bed is so wet!" she said as she landed in the water I had left on the bed from the shower.

Fortunately, the bed was still made and the comforter had caught most of the water. I asked them to stand up for a moment and I pulled all the covers off the bed leaving only the bedspread and pillows. We wouldn't need any covers, I surmised.

I sat on the bed waiting for the upcoming action. Lynn was standing facing Marilyn and slowly backed onto the bed dragging Marilyn down with her until Marilyn was laying on top of Lynn staring into her eyes. I could feel the nervousness of Marilyn as she was visibly shaking. Lynn sensed it too and laughing said, "I wish I had my first time again."

Instead of pushing Marilyn down, Lynn lifted herself up to lean against the headboard which placed Marilyn's head in her lap. Lynn then spread her knees out to the sides and lifted them slightly which exposed her pussy for Marilyn who was looking at it intently, but frightened.

Again brushing the hair out of Marilyn's face, Lynn said, "You are just too cute!

"Ok, just lick me right here," she said, as she moved her hand down and spread open the top of her clit.

By this time, I had moved to the head of the bed as well to get a better view. Marilyn looked up at Lynn's face one last time. She looked terrified, but in a good way. Lynn

155

again brushed the hair from her face and smiled at her. Marilyn smiled back and then looked down at Lynn's pussy and lowered her mouth.

Her tongue came out and contacted Lynn's clit like a kid tasting a food for the first time.

Lynn giggled a little, and said, "That's good, now just lick slowly right there."

As commanded, Marilyn began to lick Lynn's clit with the broad front of her tongue in slow short strokes, as Lynn brushed her own hair back and then petted Marilyn's head in gentle fondles all the while peering straight into her eyes.

Lynn's smile was growing wider as Marilyn began to relax. "Ok honey, now lick me down a little ok? Don't you want to taste me a little more?"

Marilyn nodded her head while never letting her tongue retract and moved down until her nose was sitting on Lynn's pelvis. The motion of her head told me she was going for it, sticking her tongue inside Lynn.

Lynn began to moan. "Oh, you are doing good honey. Can you do it faster?"

Marilyn's head began to swing back as she lunged her tongue forward deep into Lynn, to which Lynn giggled, with a bit of an evil tone I thought – she had herself a little slave.

Lynn pulled her knees up more so Marilyn could sink her tongue deep inside without craning her neck as much. I knew Lynn would never reach orgasm in this way, and I believed that wasn't her goal anyway. Lynn was being turned on by this young naïve girl plunging into her pussy.

And plunging she was. Marilyn was lapping up everything she could get of Lynn. I'd never thought of straining to get my tongue that deep in a pussy before.

While Lynn's knees were still pulled toward her shoulders, she reached down and pulled her pussy lips apart.

"I want you to lick from deep in my pussy up to my clit," she commanded.

Marilyn did her best from reaching as deep into her pussy and then licking up to her clit in slow motions. As her head bounced up, I noticed her butt wiggling. She had a plump butt, like that of a 19-year-old who had yet to develop a weight problem but teetering dangerously close. It looked soft and inviting and I became disinterested in the action between Lynn's legs.

I moved between Marilyn's legs practically unnoticed and with my dick erect over Marilyn's bouncing ass, I realized the condom was all the way across the bed in the drawer. But, I also realized zero attention was being placed on me, though I'm sure they both knew I had made my move. I reached down to check Marilyn's pussy and it was dripping.

I mounted myself over Marilyn and let my bare dick come in contact with Marilyn's crack so there would be no surprise what was about to happen. For a moment, I felt guilty that I was about to enter her uncovered, but that didn't last long. I slipped my dick next to her pussy and with a soft push slid easily inside. As soon as I did, her hips lifted in reaction and I could hear a muffled moan from Lynn's pussy, but she continued to lick with the same ferocity.

I began fucking Marilyn slowly so as not to disturb her other duties and then I caught Lynn's glare. She was scowling at me, and I could read her thoughts plainly. *You fucking asshole. You know you should use a condom.*

I shrugged at her.

"You like getting fucked while eating pussy?" I asked Marilyn.

"Ummhmmm, I love it," she answered, with a tone of being in a trance.

I looked at Lynn with a see-she-doesn't-care look, and

Lynn reluctantly dropped her scowl and focused again on her pussy getting eaten.

"Ok honey, I know it's hard to eat pussy while getting fucked. Just try to lick my clit, and let Nate fucking you move your tongue."

Lynn stretched her legs out sideways almost flat and relaxed back on the bed letting out a contented sigh, as I began to fuck Marilyn a little faster. Marilyn was doing her best to keep her tongue on Lynn's clit, who had given up the instructions and was now leaning back with her eyes closed enjoying it.

After a few minutes of fucking, I was still not satisfied with the night. The excitement of it didn't live up to the night with Athena and Jody. I felt the need to push things further or else I was going to nut inside this girl without a feeling that it was any different than the countless other nights with prostitutes.

With my hand, I moved Marilyn's left leg up so her ass was a little more exposed and then I collapsed down on top of her. I grabbed the back of her head to turn her toward me and stuck my tongue in her mouth tasting Lynn's juices and exciting Marilyn who returned the kiss passionately.

As she was sucking on my tongue with my dick still gently fucking her, I moved my hand down to her ass and caressed her butt cheeks while slowly inching my fingers toward her asshole. As my dry finger contacted her hole, I waited for any negative reaction but she responded with intensified sucking, it was exciting her. I moved my finger to her pussy to grab a bit of lubrication and then returned to her ass.

I massaged her hole gently for several seconds and then begin to slide my middle finger in. As I felt the hard cartilage of her asshole envelope my finger, she let out a moan of pleasure and excitement.

Her ass was tight. I began to work my finger around

inside her ass while pounding her pussy with deep slow thrusts. When I could feel it had worked out enough, I began to slide another finger inside of her. She didn't balk at all. She closed her eyes, moaning softly and releasing my tongue, laid her head down on Lynn's pussy, who began petting her hair and watching with interest.

"Let's do anal," I said to her seductively as if it was some kind of love making.

Marilyn lifted her head and opened her eyes wide. I could tell in that instance she was going to let me do anything.

"You better tip her big!" Lynn yelled at me, with a bit of an upset tone. I responded with a scowl as I would have preferred to not offer without being asked.

"I will take care of you honey," I said looking at Marilyn's eyes.

"I'm scared to do," she answered. "I never think to do before."

"It'll be ok, I'll go slowly and if it hurts, I'll stop," I assured her.

"Ok," she said bashfully and laid her head back down on Lynn's pussy.

"Pffft, are you sure?" asked Lynn and then began speaking to her in Tagalog.

"Hey hey, she wants to!" I interrupted. I was not about to let Lynn take this away from me.

"Ohhh, pffft," responded Lynn and jumped up toward her purse.

She was grabbing lubricant. Lynn was the experienced girl though it did not seem to please her I had taken the night in this direction. Perhaps Marilyn was too young and naïve and too enthralled with us. Was I taking advantage of her? I didn't really care at the time. I didn't care if it hurt either, I was mad with lust at that point, with a raging hard-on and a girl willing to do whatever I desired.

Lynn returned and laid down next to Marilyn's

outstretched left leg and then slapped my arm indicating I should remove my fingers from her ass. I did and let my dick flop out of her pussy and sat up. Lynn spoke to Marilyn in Tagalog and then squirted some lubricant onto her finger and reached it to Marilyn's ass. Though it seemed almost surgical, I was even more aroused at Lynn preparing Marilyn's ass for me. Then she grabbed my dick slapping some lubricant on it.

"Ok," said Lynn and she laid down on the bed facing Marilyn and began speaking in Tagalog again and grabbed Marilyn's leg stretching her knee towards the head of the bed. The result was a gapping asshole for me. I was impressed.

Marilyn's face was terrified, but I didn't care. She was focused on Lynn who was now holding her gently.

"Go slow Nathan!" Lynn demanded.

I grabbed my cock and placed the head against her well lubricated asshole and began to push. I was shocked at the ease of which it poked in, as if her asshole sucked up the tip of my dick. In the instant I slid inside, Marilyn's whole body quivered and she let out a gasp.

"Hey fucker! Be gentle!" yelled Lynn.

I mostly ignored her. I didn't push any further but I admired the scene. Marilyn's leg was stretched upwards into Lynn's chest who was caressing Marilyn's hair again. Marilyn's eyes were wide open and her whole body was tense.

"Relax honey, if it hurts too much, just say 'stop.'" I said.

I tried to calm her, but every emotion in my body was telling me to fuck this ass until it bled. She was mine, just a hole to pleasure myself with. Though I knew that plunging all my dick inside her suddenly would likely cause a scream of agony and then a very pissed off Lynn, so I gently slid my dick in and out a few millimeters at a time.

After a minute or so, it appeared Marilyn was

beginning to relax, so I went a few millimeters more and after another minute a few more, each time extracting a jolt from Marilyn before she would relax again.

"How is it honey?" Lynn asked concerned.

Marilyn looked at her and smiled, "It's ok, I like it."

Lynn laughed. "Oh really?"

Lynn leaned forward to kiss Marilyn and slid her hand down to Marilyn's pussy under her leg. Marilyn relaxed even more and began to get lost in the moment as I continued my slow millimeter by millimeter insertion into her ass.

After a few minutes, I felt I had enough depth. My dick was about halfway inserted and Marilyn's moans were becoming louder and contained more pleasure. My brain switched from easing her ass into it to getting the satisfaction I wanted. I began to fuck her ass a little faster and my thrusts brought my dick a little deeper. I could feel my orgasm building.

In that moment, I lost myself. I slammed my hips against Marilyn's ass and grabbed her shoulders. Her whole body tensed up and she released a startled and painful gasp, but I didn't hear the word 'stop.'

I began to ram my dick in her ass as forcefully as I could as my orgasm was imminent. Marilyn's head was now buried into the bed and Lynn wrapped her arm around her back and held her tight, and I could feel the muscles in her ass flex. A tight ring of muscle closed around the opening of her asshole which I slid my dick through pleasurably.

I continued my mad thrusts. Marilyn's back was arched in tense agony as I pounded her, bringing myself to orgasm. As I erupted, I pulled back on her shoulders and dumped my semen deep in her ass twitching my hips violently as I released every drop. I then collapsed on top of Marilyn as if she wasn't even a person, I'm not sure I even remembered where I was. I was euphoric.

161

"Get the fuck off her!" yelled Lynn pushing me.

I snapped out of it and raised up. My dick flopped out of her ass along with a release of gas.

"Oh jesus," I said whiffing the fumes and removing myself to the shower for cleanup.

Returning with a clean dick a minute later, they were still laying in the same position on the bed. Marilyn was crying and Lynn was holding her. They were speaking Tagalog to each other and I knew they were not happy with me. Perhaps I was a douchebag, but at the time I felt upset they were being so emotional.

"Oh, stop, it wasn't that bad," I said jumping on the bed. Touching Marilyn's butt cheek to look at her asshole and causing a flinch.

"See not even any blood." Was I trying to be cute? *I don't really know.*

Lynn was scowling at me angrily.

Nonchalantly, I laid down on the bed and said to Marilyn, "I'm sorry if I hurt you, but that was amazing! Whatever you want, you will get it. The first time is always a little hard, but you know you can make lots of money doing this."

Marilyn raised her head and nodded through tears as if to say, "yea, I know but it really sucks."

"Ten Thousand Pesos, you better give her!" yelled Lynn.

"Jesus Fucking Christ Lynn!" I yelled back. Holy shit, I was so pissed at Lynn. It wasn't any of her business.

As Marilyn wiped away her tears and began to relax and sit up, we engaged in a negotiation. It was mostly Lynn and I negotiating while Marilyn slowly became happy with the situation. After a few minutes, we agreed on 4,000 pesos, which seemed like robbery to me, but then again, it's hard enough to find a girl to do anal, much less a young somewhat attractive girl who was eating out a pussy at the same time.

Afterward, though certainly relieved at the nice payday, I could sense Marilyn was shell-shocked and I assumed she would be more than happy to get out of there. Additionally, if she was going to act like an abused girl, I would rather she leave anyway. When I asked her if she wanted to leave, the answer was unsurprisingly yes. Lynn and she spoke for a while in Tagalog, exchanged numbers and about an hour after I had my dick in her ass, she was out the door.

WHAP!

It took a moment to comprehend what had just happened. I closed the door behind Marilyn and turning around felt a stinging sensation on my face. Perplexed, I was staring into the fuming scowl of Lynn. She had slapped me with every bit of strength she had.

"How could you do that? She's just a girl!" yelled Lynn.

Years of bargirls, and there is always something new to experience. I had just ass fucked a girl fresh off the bus and then gotten slapped by a bargirl who'd obviously been rode hard and had some resentments for it.

I smiled.

"Oh Jesus Lynn, don't be all OA[22]," I said dismissing her and heading to the bathroom. I stood in front of the mirror with my phone waiting to see if a red mark appeared.

"I'm not OA! You scared her!" she continued.

"So what? She could have said 'stop' at any time," I reasoned.

"No, she's only girl. You are man," she said.

---

[22] OA – Overacting. Filipino expression, when someone is making a big deal about nothing.

The reality is that Lynn was very much correct in this. I did take advantage of Marilyn, all the while excusing it because she was a bargirl. Maybe I was no better than the Japanese man next door. I didn't feel the least bit guilty though. In fact, I was utterly fulfilled in how the night went. My thirst for debauchery was quenched thoroughly. That urge that had built up for months at home and that I was looking for those last few nights scouring the bars with Lynn was gone. 4,000 pesos? I would have given 50,000 if I had known the satisfaction it would bring me.

Watching a small red mark appear on my cheek, I could not hold back a grin from also appearing. As I snapped a pic smiling madly, I laughed.

"Lynn, what do you want me to say? I don't see what the problem is. How about you and I do anal tomorrow?"

"Ughh! See how you are!" she said and stormed off.

I leaned against the sink and thought, "Ok, well, now what?"

The guy in the mirror was a champion. He'd done everything in life now, there were no more bucket lists. The vacation could end at that moment and it would be the best sex excursion ever.

CHAPTER 12

A Lunatic in Love

Lynn's little tirade was short-lived and she again acted the girlfriend while staying the night with me. I'm sure she didn't want to disrupt her daily stipend over a girl she'd just met anyway. Awaking with her under my arm after a night of fun with another bargirl was becoming normal. That was my world and I saw no reason to cut it short – shorter than it already would be anyway as I only had a week left.

In fact, as we went through the motions of breakfast and hanging out at the hotel pool, the events of the previous night weren't even brought up. She really didn't care. The emotion of the moment caused her to be upset with me, but I'm sure she'd heard of much worse in her time, maybe even witnessed much worse.

For me though, the guilt was beginning to fester. I'd always thought of myself as the nice guy that picked up poor bargirls and showed them a better time than any of their other customers. I was a gentleman that treated them as I would any woman anywhere in the world. It was a sobering morning for me realizing what I had in me. I've heard men talk of that sort of night, pushing harder and harder so long as the girl doesn't fight back.

My guilt was not in that I felt ashamed. It was the opposite, I felt empowered, as if finally getting that fix I craved from these sex trips. The desire I had to push boundaries had controlled every action. I had blindly fought to fulfill myself and didn't bother to consider the feelings of Marilyn or Lynn. On future trips, would it happen again and how far might I go? What is after rough anal sex with an inexperienced bargirl?

I allowed myself some consolation though. Marilyn never said "stop," even though I had coached her to do so. I wondered if I would have stopped. As my orgasm was imminent while plowing my dick into her ass and she yelled "stop," would I have been able to ease up? I didn't even know. My memories of that moment were foggy, like a drunken episode even though I had had only a few beers.

The verdict, however, is that no one could accuse me of being the same as the Japanese guy I interrupted several nights previously, who continued to push despite the pleas to stop. Marilyn had simply dug her head into the bed in order to take it, and that period was short-lived. From the time I began hurting her to nutting in her ass was less than a few minutes.

If I kept making these excuses to myself, would I finally be ok with it? I hoped not. I wanted the previous night to be a onetime experience, I didn't want to be one of those sex tourists.

"I need to go home this afternoon, but can I meet you for dinner?" asked Lynn as we returned from the pool.

This was music to my ears. For the last several days, Lynn had rarely left my side, and I had wanted it that way as she was my partner in crime. Now that the crime had been committed, I was ready for some alone time.

She gathered some of her things, but left most of her makeup and such when I confirmed dinner with her. I'd normally want a short fuck session with her before she left, but I was fulfilled. I don't believe the thought even crossed my mind.

Sitting alone in the room, I felt like a different man. The events before meeting Lynn seemed like a distant memory. I needed this time to recharge. That afternoon, I went back to Body Bliss Massage, took a short nap, and simply relaxed in my room, waiting for Lynn's text in the evening.

By the time Lynn's text came at around 8pm, I was bored and ready for a night out. We agreed to meet at Chow King which was halfway between the hotel and SM Mall. Lynn was getting a little spoiled, but I didn't feel like spending a ton of money on food after the handout the night before.

I made my way out the hotel and toward the perimeter. It was a slow mid-week night and it felt gloomy. The excitement was gone for me as I passed the door girls at Tropix and Las Vegas clubs. The city seemed like it had nothing left to offer me. Perhaps tonight, we'd just hang out at Gossip. None of these girls could do anything for me.

It's ok to follow your heart on a sex vacation.

As I began approaching the Perimeter area, I remembered Jenny. She should be outside the door of her bar at this early hour bringing customers in. I wouldn't mind getting a hug from her being the first time I was out of Lynn's company. I looked for that sexy hourglass black dress, but it was missing.

Sitting on a box with her back turned by the door was a girl with the same blonde highlights as Jenny, though. Could that be her? She was wearing a set of high-end street clothes. The outfit was mostly grey with a yellow design, with shorts and a matching shirt that covered her shoulders. I could just make out her short fair-skinned legs crossed on the other side of the box. She was conversing with the cherry girl, who was in a black dress at work.

167

That was definitely Jenny, but she was not working.

I walked up quickly and leaned on the box grinning like a fool.

"AHHHHH!" she screamed. Her face lit up like a girl at the altar when she saw me.

"I've missed you so much!" she said as she stood up and threw her arms around my neck.

My heart missed a beat as I held her in the air for a moment with my face smothered in her freshly-washed hair that smelled like mangoes. She swayed as she tightened the hold on my neck and to me, nothing else existed in the world.

"Your friend is an asshole!" she said finally as I dropped her.

"Who? John?" I asked. I had not seen John since High Society and oh right! The cherry girl!

"What happened?" I asked, looking at the girl John had left with. Somehow, she seemed a little more mature.

The girl shook her head. "Where is John?" she asked.

I instantly knew what had happened. John had managed to pop her cherry, probably telling her how much he cared, and then had promptly dumped her and gone back to his new fiancé. I remembered Jenny telling me the same kind of story for her first time. Why is it so hard for these girls to hold out for 100,000 pesos?

"I haven't seen John myself since that night. You know he is engaged right?" I asked thinking I might as well sever any hope she may have had.

"He's what?!" Jenny asked incredulous.

"Hey, I'm sorry Jenny. He's not a good friend or anything, I only just met him," I said.

The ex-cherry girl shook her head and shrugged. I wondered what upset her more, that she lost her virginity in a one night stand or that she could no longer get a 100,000 peso bonus for it. And… I had to find John later!

Jenny looked at me trying to act upset, but I'm not

sure if she's even capable of it. Her positive personality showed through the forced frown on her face. I chuckled at her and she immediately dropped the frown and grinned at me.

"Where are you going?" she asked.

"Chow King," I replied.

"Oh! I want Chow King!" she exclaimed happily and grabbed my arm as if to lead me there.

"Jenny, I can't right now," I answered reactively.

"Oh pfft!" she smirked, released my arm and returned to her seat on the box, never showing any real disappointment.

I looked at her on the box trying to act hurt. She couldn't pull it off, it's as if she didn't know how to show a negative emotion. She was possibly the loveliest girl I'd ever met.

Knowing I had promised to meet Lynn, I turned around and began to walk away, but in the first few steps, a wave of emotion and thought came over me. I didn't want to be with anyone else besides Jenny at that moment. It seemed like I had two choices for the rest of my trip. I could be the line-stepping sex tourist with Lynn, or I could be young-again and in-love with Jenny. Prior to the night with Marilyn, I likely would have chosen Lynn, but not now. I stopped in my tracks as it was no choice for me, I desired only Jenny. The real decision was whether I would stand Lynn up. She didn't deserve to be stood up, but at the same time, I didn't owe her anything.

It's ok to follow your heart on a sex vacation. So, sorry to all my readers who would like to hear of more debauchery, but the rest of my trip was pretty sappy. Romance on a sex vacation? It is more common than you'd think.

I turned around and walked back towards Jenny, whose face lit up in delight. She jumped off the box and ran to me wrapping her arms around my waist.

"So, do you want Chow King or Jollibee?" I asked. *They always want Jollibee.*

"Oh! Jollibee! I want Jollibee!" she exclaimed happily.

I put my arm around her and kept going the opposite direction from Chow King.

"Hey, Jollibee right there," Jenny said pointing toward a Jollibee that sits across from the Chow King where Lynn was going.

"Oh I know, but isn't the other one our favorite?" I asked her.

She giggled.

"You are not working tonight?" I asked.

"No, no work tonight. I'm all yours for free!" she laughed.

As we made our way toward Walking Street embracing each other so at times it was difficult to keep my balance, I realized the trip had taken a major turn and there would be more heartbreak for me than if I had kept going to the rendezvous with Lynn. I was in love with Jenny, I could feel it throughout my body. It certainly had something to do with having my ego fulfilled the night before, it's as if all the bullshit had been stripped away and I was now willing to be a caring man.

It scared me. I've felt it before with a bargirl, but it was crippling with Jenny. Just thinking that I'd soon have to go home caused sharp heartburn. I tried to put that out of my mind and enjoy the time with her.

Then there was Lynn, I couldn't just stand her up completely. I stopped to text her, "Sorry, I can't make it to Chow King." I thought that was enough, but I'd forgotten about her things still in the room.

Jollibee was more than busy. It seemed the whole city

decided to have a late dinner.

Besides the Choco Crunch[23], I don't care much for the food there, and adding that it's always busy with loud families making it impossible to eat in peace, I would skip it. However, when it comes to making Filipinas happy, there is no better cost-effective solution. It's roughly as cheap as eating street food, but every Filipina would rather eat Jollibee than a luxury sit down restaurant. Other cheap fast food such as McDonalds or KFC simply don't elicit the same kind of excitement.

As an American, the lack of seating would make one panic, but Jenny found two seats at the end of a table that was being used by a large family. She sat down without even acknowledging the family, which is perfectly acceptable behavior in the Philippines where public places are often packed and personal space is wholly unimportant.

Things were a little awkward for me, knowing that a middle-aged Filipino father next to me seemed to be listening to our every word, even over the screams of his children.

"Why you not come see me? You have other girl, don't you?" asked Jenny in a manner like she didn't truly care. It was just a fact of life in Angeles City.

"Uhhh"

Jenny chuckled.

Then my phone beeped. Ah shit, why didn't I turn it on vibrate?

"She misses you already," laughed Jenny. "Is she pretty?"

I was sensing a bit of jealousy, but as is usually the case with Jenny, she remained in her positive attitude.

"You are the prettiest girl in Angeles I think," I answered.

---

[23] Choco Chrunch – 25 cent ice cream with chocolate. I could eat 10 of them.

My phone beeped again.

"You can call her."

I rolled my eyes and took out my phone to check the messages obviously from Lynn and to put it on vibrate. The two messages from Lynn were "Why" and "Where are you?" Though probably not the best choice, I decided to ignore her.

"Do you want me to leave?" asked Jenny.

"No way," I answered. "I'm glad I saw you, you are the nicest and prettiest girl I've met here."

Jenny smiled, and then shrugged her shoulders, as I realized my mistake. Even though I said she was the best, I still made it clear there were many others.

"How many girlfriends do you have?" she asked.

Oops. This is a conversation that cannot be won and I had to figure a way out of it.

My phone vibrated. It was loud enough in Jollibee that Jenny was not aware.

"I don't want any girlfriend except you. In fact, do you want to get married?" I joked. *Wait, what?*

Jenny's face brightened up in delight and giggles. "Yes, please! I want to marry you!"

Shit, let's go back to the previous conversation.

My phone vibrated again and I instinctively looked down and toward the pocket where my phone was, and when lifting my eyes caught the gaze of the Filipino man who had a slight smirk as if to say, "Lucky dog."

"How many days do you have off?" I asked her.

"Only one. But I will stay with you as long as you want," was her reply.

I was happy about her response. Did she mean for free? I needed to find out if she expected me to pay the barfine every day. I probably would have, but if I could get out of it, even better.

"Won't you get fired?" I asked.

"It's ok. Many bars."

She truly liked me. She wanted to stay with me without the care of getting paid for it. As I had thought before, her main goal in working in Angeles City was to find a husband, not to make money as a bargirl. For me, it was a win-win situation. I liked her and wanted to spend the rest of my time in Angeles City with her, but now it was not going to cost me a nightly barfine, in stark contrast to my days with Lynn that I had to pay multiple barfines on some nights along with a fee to Lynn.

"I would love that," I said, smiling.

Jenny smiled bashfully, as did the Filipino man next to her, and my phone vibrated again.

For the next 20 minutes, we sat at Jollibee enjoying our cheap hamburgers and ice cream and each other's company, including the man who at times had short Tagalog conversations with Jenny. They seemed to be planning my demise as a bachelor. All the while my phone continued to vibrate. Lynn was obviously very upset, but I didn't think there was anything to be done about it.

We left and made our way slowly back to Central Park. Leaving Jollibee, we had our arms around each other and it felt as if we had agreed to be in a monogamous relationship, like two college kids. I was thrilled that despite the events of my little trip, I could still feel that way towards a girl. I had a crush as if I was 20 years-old.

Shit.

Looking back on it, the situation could have been avoided if I had simply checked my phone. Holding the lobby door of Central Park open for Jenny, my stomach twisted as I made eye contact with Lynn sitting on the lobby sofa. Jenny, naturally oblivious, walked toward the elevator as I carefully stepped into the lobby not sure what events would follow.

Lynn stood up, scrunched her mouth, and then shook her head disappointedly as she walked towards me. I was focused on Jenny who at any time would become aware of the situation.

"I need my things," Lynn said calmly. "She's very beautiful."

Shit.

Jenny was now standing in the foyer with her hands on her waist and I believe it may have been the first time I saw her with a true scowl. I was terrified and practically unable to move. Though they were both bargirls, Jenny no longer felt like one to me. It's as if my girlfriend had caught me with a hooker.

"Ok," I said collecting myself and walking toward Jenny and the elevators.

"Jenny, I'm sorry, can you wait here for two minutes?" I said as her face went from confused to devastated.

"No no, it's ok honey," said Lynn to Jenny. "Come up with us, it will only take a minute."

Jenny stood motionless.

I sighed, knowing this night could end badly and I might even end up spending it with Lynn again. I pushed the button hoping Jenny didn't make a dash for the front door.

The elevator could not have arrived any slower. When one finally opened and we waited for a group of Asians with their bargirls to pour out, the three of us thankfully strode in. Jenny stood against the wall turned away from us with an "I hate this" look on her face. I didn't know what to do, except wait until I was alone with her again.

Finally, Lynn broke the silence in the elevator by speaking to Jenny in Tagalog, and before we arrived on my floor, the usual charm of Lynn managed to turn the corners of Jenny's mouth when she replied to her in

174

English, "Yes."

I would have loved to understand what Lynn said, but I'll just have to settle with the thought that Lynn said something to the tune of, "He is an amazing man isn't he?" Though it was probably something like, "He's not cheap like most guys."

Finally, we were in the room. Jenny went straight for the chair by the window and looked out ignoring us. Lynn went into the bathroom to gather her things while I stood guard at the bathroom door to usher her out as quickly as possible.

As Lynn was standing at the sink, she looked up to see me standing on guard and her expression turned from emotionless to melancholy. She continued to pack up her things but I could see tears forming in her eyes. All this time, I'd thought of Lynn as a professional, it was surprising for me to see emotion in her.

She finished packing up her makeup bag and stopped to wipe the wetness away from her face. Then she stood in the mirror for a moment to look at me. The sight of Lynn's sadness had changed my own expression from one of stoic problem-solver to caring ex. She smiled understandingly and turned to head toward the door.

"It's ok Nate. You know I'll be here if it doesn't work out with her." And with that, Lynn was gone.

Before I could approach Jenny for damage reduction, I had to clear the choke from my throat. What was that emotion I saw in Lynn? Was it simply the hurt of being exchanged for a younger girl or was it something more? Did she have feelings for me?

It was jarring. Lynn had shown me a wonderful time, probably the best few days I've ever had on a sex vacation. It was not only the sex acts she was willing to engage in, but also her charm. In reality, I WAS throwing her away for a younger more beautiful girl. I felt I should have been more considerate of Lynn, I had just treated her as a fired

175

employee only allowed to enter the bathroom to get her personal effects... *which she was.*

Oh, for fuck's sake... she's just a hooker, I tried to tell myself. Though in the Philippines, they simply don't feel like hookers.

I walked to Jenny, knelt down behind the chair and wrapped my arms around her shoulders not saying anything. Her face was blank. That was probably the look she has when upset.

"How many girls do you have?" she asked.

"Now? Only you. I promise."

Waiting for a girl to get over her emotions so I can bang her is an agonizing task. She was staying with me for free, so I felt I shouldn't pressure her, instead I was forced to wait like a boyfriend who'd just got caught talking to his ex.

After what felt like an eternity (only 5 minutes probably), she moved from the chair to the bed. Though still fully clothed, we slipped under the covers together and flipped through the TV channels. Or... more to the point, she flipped through them until she found a silly Philippine game show in Tagalog. I guess knocking down stacked coke cans with rubber bands is a thing? She enjoyed it though and I assumed her laughter would get us closer to doing the deed.

She watched the rubber band coke can game for a millennia (I'd guess 20 minutes). When it was over, she started flipping channels again, as I moved in close to her and hoped she wouldn't find another ridiculous gameshow to watch.

Though still on her back, I leaned forward for a kiss. Thankfully, she turned to me and allowed me to move in all the way, though she didn't return the kiss. I had the embarrassing experience of kissing lips that did not move. She was still pouting.

She turned back to flipping channels and again managed to find some cock-blocking gameshow. This time it was children having a balloon race. Jenny again opened up in laughter ignoring me while I tried to scooch in closer.

The infiniteness of this children competing with parlor tricks gameshow was easily the worst 15 minutes of the trip. I tried to focus on feeling Jenny's amazing body under her clothes as she ignored me, but it wasn't enough. Especially with this hard-to-get-because-you-did-something-bad game she was playing, I wanted her so much it was hurting. My dick had been hard for 20 minutes and I knew she could feel it. How could she be so insensitive?

I leaned in for another kiss when she started flipping channels again, and to my delight she turned to me and giggled. That seemed like a signal that she was now satisfied with the punishment she had given me.

She dropped the remote and wrapped her arm around my head and laid a big smooch on me. Then she ran her hand down to my dick and massaged it through my pants.

"I'm your only girl now, right?" she asked.

"I promise."

Jenny then pushed the covers off her and began removing her clothes. She pulled her shirt off and her frizzled highlighted hair covered her seductive smile. She removed her bra and then pulled her shorts and panties off in one quick motion.

I was lost in the pleasure of watching the beauty that was unmasked for me. She turned on her side, propped her head on her elbow and raised her top knee in the air exposing her shaved pussy. She was smiling playfully.

I began to undo my pants...

"Wait," she said. "You owe me."

"What do you mean?"

She giggled and began to crawl toward the top of the bed. Then placing one knee next to my shoulder and balancing on the headboard, she extended her hips over my face and dropped her other knee across me. She gently lowered her pussy down to my mouth.

Was this supposed to be a punishment? Cause it wasn't. It was more like a reward. I grabbed her soft hips with my hands and pulled her body down on my mouth to give my tongue all the pressure I could in massaging her clit. All the while, I never took my eyes off that young body with perfect breasts stretched out above me. She continued bracing herself against the headboard alternating between looking down into my eyes and looking up to the ceiling to moan.

Lying there totally relaxed with this young beautiful girl's pussy squashed in my mouth, I felt as if everything was now perfect in my life. I wanted to relive this experience every day. I wanted to make Jenny the happiest girl on the planet... especially if this is what made her happy.

As her moans became faster, she began to slide her hips back and forth over my mouth with her clit rubbing from under my nose down to my chin. She was getting wetter from my spit and her own juices and the mixture began to dribble down the sides of my mouth. And she grinded faster as I attempted to keep my tongue attached to her clit to pleasure her in the best way I knew how. *She never even smashed my tongue against my teeth.*

The view of her tiny body dancing directly above my eyes was a sight I'll never forget. There was not a blemish anywhere from her hips across her fair skinned flat Asian belly, over her perfectly proportioned breasts with small hard nipples and up to her face which was now staring down at me with a look of aphrodisia.

She continued her lustful stare through squinted eyelids as she continued grinding my face and her moans became louder and more frequent. Finally, as she climaxed, she grabbed my hair with one hand and braced herself with the other on the headboard and mashed her pussy into me with all her weight. I slowly massaged her clit with the fat portion of my tongue, until she smiled and relaxed.

Still not moving her pussy from my mouth, she leaned back and sat her weight on her heels, and brushed her hair back giving me the greatest smile of satisfaction. Then she began petting my hair with both hands as she held her pussy on my tongue. With her hair back and her body arched and satisfied with that beautiful smile on her face, I was in heaven.

"Thank you, honey," she said after staring at me for a good minute.

Jenny then leaned back and began undoing my belt and pants, though I could not wait for that. I hurriedly removed my pants, even with her pussy still sitting on my mouth.

Then with one graceful motion, she slid back taking me entirely inside her.

I was ready to blow almost instantly. In the most passionate session of intercourse so far on my trip, our bodies moved in unison as I slid in and out of her tight lubricated pussy. I tried to hold back my orgasm as long as I could, but when she dropped her body down on me and smashed her tongue in my mouth, I erupted.

As my cum filled her, she flexed her thighs tightly around me and sucked on my upper lip while moaning in pure joy, and after I finished, she collapsed on me and laid her head on my shoulder wrapping her arms around my neck, never letting me slip out of her soaked vagina.

"I love you," she whispered in my ear.

"I love you, too."

What did I say?
Shit.

CHAPTER 13

Saying Goodbyes

The sightseeing around Angeles City pleasantly surprised even me. I've been vacationing there for almost 10 years and until this trip never knew there were hot springs and mud spas, or lay down sand pits, or something. They called it a wellness spa, I called it getting buried with ugly sand and having goop rubbed on your face for 3000 pesos.

They had a 4x4 jeep for rent though! This was a highlight of the trip. To get to the sand pits, they gave me a 4x4 to drive! Through water and mud! The guide that was with us was not at all happy with the way I drove. Jenny was thrilled though! She loved it. Every time the jeep lurched as I took a corner too fast or drove purposely over an obstacle, she screamed and laughed like a teenager on a roller-coaster. I could take her to America and be confident she wouldn't bitch about my driving. Was there anything about her I didn't see as perfect?

I enjoyed the hot springs the most, especially since Jenny stripped down to her skimpy bikini I'd bought her for the trip and all the Asian sex tourists in the springs drooled as I had brought the most beautiful one by far.

Then it was Mt Pinatubo. For years, I'd been waiting for an excuse to visit the newly created lake in the caldera of the mountain that blew its top in the early 90s. The volcano devastated the surrounding country and older Filipinos remember it as a life altering catastrophe. I've seen documentaries of it and I can't imagine the hardships these already poor people would have faced. That said, it was a beautiful lake and a peaceful little daytrip. I'd say I overpaid at 4,000 pesos each, I should have shopped around.

Then there was shopping, and eating out, and more shopping. I was spoiling Jenny just like an idiot sex tourist, and most of it was my idea. Every day, it seemed she would have been happy with hanging at the hotel pool and eating Jollibee. For some reason, I felt unsuitable for Jenny. She was a sexy highly desirable angel and the only way to earn her love was to buy it – this unfortunately was probably true, even if she didn't know it herself.

The day before leaving Angeles City, I asked Jim to meet me at the SM Clark food court while I gave Jenny some money to buy a special going-away dress for the night's activities. I relayed the experiences of my sex trip to him.

"I'm crazy about this girl, Jim. I've never felt this way about any bargirl before."

The ridicule in Jim's tone and expression was hard to miss. He knew this story, he'd heard it many times from men in Angeles.

"I don't know, it sounds like Lynn is the special one. She seems like a keeper. What's Jenny going to do for you? Besides take all your money," he mocked.

"Surely you've fallen for one of these girls before?" I asked.

"Fell for? Never. I've cared about many of them but have I loved one so much I was willing to risk everything for her? No.

"Maybe you do love her, I don't know. Or maybe she's just a young sexy little spinner that makes your dick harder than any of the others," he said. "And don't forget, they are whores. They didn't come to Angeles City to find love, they came here to find a way out."

"I wish I lived here like you," I said. "Is this the real reason you moved here? So you could be with one of them without getting married?"

"Oh man, you're really fucked up right now. Not even

the same Nate I knew two weeks ago. You know it's only been two weeks, right?

"I moved here to fuck young sexy spinners one after the other, not to marry one," he said.

Jim's reasoning ringed true in my ears. What could I really know about a girl in two weeks?

"And you're cumming inside her?" Jim continued his little rant. "So, I know a girl that got pregnant by a Canadian asshole who told her he loved her... yada yada... 8 months into the pregnancy, he disappeared off all social media. Is that what you are going to do to Jenny?

"Or are you going to send her and the baby money every month for years?"

I became exasperated at the thought of some asshole knocking up Jenny and then leaving her in Angeles City to fend for herself. Could I be the asshole? The thought of sending money for the next couple decades certainly wasn't a more pleasant thought. I had been choosing to not think about that. Every day for almost a week I'd been cumming in Jenny without asking her if she was on the pill or even what time of the month it was.

The dread of Jenny getting pregnant was enough to change my outlook on the relationship. I cringed at the idea that Jenny would contact me on Facebook in a couple weeks to tell me she was pregnant. I obviously wasn't truly in love with her. As Jim said it, she just made my dick harder than any of the other bargirls.

Up until my lunch with Jim, my heart was moving in the direction of asking Jenny to marry me at the end of the trip. Would I have done it? I have no idea. I've gone on these trips many times and never once thought of doing anything but leaving all the girls behind when I went home. After this talk, I began to move my brain (and dick) in that direction. As Jenny approached us in the food court with a bag containing her new dress, she looked slightly more like a girl I'd never see again come tomorrow.

"Well Nate, if you're going to fall for one, you sure picked a good one," Jim said after I made introductions.

Jenny smiled, patted Jim on the shoulder, and said, "Thank you sir!"

A bit of jealousy crept into me during that exchange between Jim and Jenny. Soon, he'd be all alone in that city with her and possibly the only requirement for them sleeping together is if he ponied up 2,000 pesos. My brain was seriously going wacko...

I said goodbye to Jim, expecting I'd see him again in several months. Jenny and I made our way back to the hotel to see her in her new dress. She must like yellow. She picked out a long elegant yellow dress that matched her highlights. She looked amazing and my heart fluttered yet again.

Then we had sex... and I cummed in her yet again. *Zero Control.*

That night, I managed to schedule a time to meet up with John. He was at his hotel, the Wild Orchid, having dinner with his fiancé. I told Jenny to wait in the room to avoid any awkwardness.

It was obvious within five minutes why he'd been so hard to pin down over the last week. His fiancé had discovered his little tryst with the cherry girl and had forbid him to do anything without her. I thought at times during our dinner she had his nuts wrenched in her hand under the table.

I sat at that table for over an hour, wasting valuable time I could be spending with Jenny, until finally she decided to go to the room. "Ok, you stay here, honey?" she asked John, more of a command I thought.

"We'll be right here getting drunk," replied John.

Finally, I was alone with John and could not contain my anticipation.

"You fucked that cherry girl? What the hell? And got caught?" I asked.

John's face finally turned from man on the end of a whip to exhilarated sex tourist. John wasn't the type of man to get married any more than I was. He lived for the conquests and admiration the girls give him just because of his money. His wife was just a Jenny: a girl that made his dick harder than any of the others and was now getting a free ride to America for it.

"Oh man, it was a crazy night! I gave up some freedom, but it was so worth it!" he said.

"You would not believe how crazy that little plump cherry girl was," he said in a fit of laughter. "She'd sucked a ton of dicks in her cherry girl career, and she was ready for dick in her cunt. I dropped my load inside her twice. Red cum soup the first time, but she wanted it again."

"But how? Why'd she do it? Did you get her wasted?" I asked.

"Not too drunk, I promise... well, definitely not as drunk as me anyway. Probably why my dumb ass got another room at this same hotel where my girl was," he laughed.

I couldn't help but laugh with him in ridicule.

"I guess you should have just used the same room where your wife was," I said.

"Yeah... Fiancé... so anyway....

"We're dancing at High Society, and my dick is harder than a baseball bat. I'm keeping it on her so she can feel it while we are grinding.

"Out of nowhere, she reaches her hand down my pants and starts jerking me off right on the dance floor. I can't do anything but stand there. Well, apparently they aren't real tolerant of guys getting jerked off in the middle of the dance floor," he laughed.

185

The image was hysterical to me: A big middle-aged western man standing still in the middle of High Society with a barely-18 chubby virgin's hand down his pants just stroking it, just going to town on his dick while fellow sex tourists and Filipinos party all around. I wonder if security was rude when they shuffled him out or if they did the polite tap on the shoulder.

"So, we're walking down Walking Street towards my hotel and she is tucked under my arm continuing to stroke me under my pants."

I pictured John with some clownish smile on his face while the crowd turned their heads at them. He wasn't the type of guy to give a shit at the public display. He probably would have considered it a badge of honor.

"We get to Santos Street and she says to me, 'I want to blowjob you.' Well, I'm still in a decent state of mind at this point and I know I can't take her to my hotel and I thought I could just take her into a Blow-row bar. It worked, though I had to take some ugly skank in the room with me. I ended up getting two blowjobs, one from the cherry girl who didn't seem to give a shit, and one from a toothless whore that wouldn't have been able to get me hard otherwise."

The logistics of what John accomplished boggled my mind. Some of the bars on Santos Street have little back rooms where you can get a cheap blowjob, but I wouldn't expect them to let any girl off the street to come in and blow someone. I guess he worked it out by also paying one of their girls, all the while this cherry girl is so horny she doesn't care about being treated like a piece of trash.

"Woh, wait," I said. "So, why did you end up at the hotel anyway?"

"Well, first off, I get hammered at that little bar. They sold me over 5 shots in ten minutes, and I'm totally disgusting. I'm sweaty and I smelled like a toilet down there. I still got my blowjobs but I know it's bad... and I don't get off, and after 15 minutes or so, I tell her I want a shower and ask her if she'll keep going. She couldn't be more eager... and things start getting fuzzy at that point."

John managed to turn a chubby cherry girl on so much in High Society that he got her to blow him with some skank in a Blow-row bar and then go to his room where he fucked her twice without a condom, because as he put it, "she's a virgin, why the fuck would I wear a condom?" He told me bits and pieces of his time in that hotel room, at least the bits he could remember, and it's every bit as raunchy as sessions I've had with highly experienced bargirls. Those details are for another time...

Why the fuck was John getting married? I thought about that, I wouldn't want to be the John dragging around the weighted chain, I wanted to be the John getting blowjobs from a cherry girl and toothless whore in an Angeles City Blow-row bar backroom.

John and I sat at the Wild Orchid for another hour or so bullshitting. He swore he loved his fiancé and didn't mean to cheat on her with the cherry girl, and certainly not with some Blow-row skank. He even jokingly tried to blame me for barfining her. John seemed content that he was done with Angeles City. I could only think that he'd be back in a few years when his wife left him in America.

I said goodbye, not really thinking I'd never see him again. He was a Sex Excursionist, the same as me. I had a Jim to talk sense into me, and I guess Allen was wholly inadequate in that department. I tried for a moment saying, "When you could have a night like that, why the hell would you get married?" but John was stoic and focused on walking down the aisle.

Good luck to you, John.

Either break it off at the end of the trip or marry her.

While I made the short journey from Wild Orchid back to Central Park, I made peace with myself on what the next 24-hours would bring. The feelings I had for Jenny were real, I loved her, but I was not ready to risk bringing a girl to America and hoping she stayed with me for more than 2 years. Besides that, I craved my little sex excursions two or three times per year, and I'd never had an experience like John's. Yes, I persuaded a new bargirl to eat pussy and get her ass cummed in, but I'd never banged a cherry girl for free, or even not-for-free. Was that my next conquest?

My stomach would churn when I thought of leaving Jenny though. I had not made her any promises, but I didn't want to leave her in a lurch... the cowardice act of letting a girl think you were going to see her again, while never intending to. I cared about her too much for that. I have a rule when I get close to a girl on these sex trips: Either break it off at the end of the trip or marry her.

There are many reasons for this rule, such as the baggage that comes with a long distance relationship. The girls will all expect you to keep talking to them and most will expect you to send money. They all will ask for it. Then there is the jealousy that goes both ways. They are bargirls, they will be with other men, but they'll lie about it. She will also ask about your relationships and snoop around your social media. But the main reason is peace of mind. Let them get on with their bargirl life without having to hide anything, and let yourself be the sex tourist that you are, so that on your next trip you won't have any obligations. If all you want is to see them on your next vacation, I promise you, it doesn't matter if you keep a long distance relationship, just keep a way to get in touch. It's way cheaper.

The flip side of that rule is if you truly care about her, then saddle up and marry her, why fuck around? What can you learn about her through months of online dating anyway? You'll never truly know how she feels about you until she gets her permanent green card, so get on with it, before another sex tourist beats you to it.

I've had the talk at the end of numerous sex trips, but none of them were with a girl that I felt the same as I did with Jenny. I dreaded the next day when I would say goodbye and tell her I would probably not see her again, but I was resigned to doing exactly that. I wouldn't think about it again the rest of the night, though. I wanted one last wonderful night with a girl who felt like my true love. And... I was going to cum inside her as many times as I could manage. What difference would it make at that point?

That vow couldn't stop my heart from flopping around again when she opened the door, wearing the same yellow shirt and jean shorts she wore the first night I barfined her. She smiled and threw her arms around my chest.

"I missed you honey." she said. "I'm hungry!"

"Room service," I said. I had that answer prepared. The rest of the night was going to be spent right in the room.

The last night with Jenny was euphoric at times and painful at other times. I dropped my semen in her three times, never quite able to dismiss the thought that I could be getting her pregnant. I decided not to bring up the subject of whether she was on birth control. Just knowing the odds of her getting pregnant would not change whether she was likely to, and she probably wasn't on it anyway, none of them are, it's against their catholic upbringing.

She seemed ecstatic with every load. My brain, or maybe it was my dick, wanted to propose to her as I slid in and out. It was a constant battle to control those urges.

During the third and final session, I was ready to be out of Angeles City and done with it. I cared about her too much, but knowing there would be no future with her, it was simply too painful.

She was the most beautiful person I've ever been with, and I still love her to this day.

I awoke the morning of my scheduled departure from Angeles City staring into the weeping eyes of Jenny. She'd maintained her usual cheer the whole week right up until this point, but now it seemed she was going to be an emotional wreck.

My plan was to catch an afternoon bus from Angeles and spend one night at the Victoria Court in Manila before catching my early flight back to reality. We'd had a long night and I didn't wake up until 11am, it was already time to start getting packed up... and it was time to tell her to forget about me.

I grabbed her neck and pulled her in tight to me while still lying in bed. This was going to be harsh.

"Jenny, I had such an amazing time with you. You are the most charming girl I've ever met. Someday soon, you are going to make a man very happy," I said, as my own tears started to flow.

Her body went motionless as I said those words, and then after a few seconds, she broke down and cried.

"I love you so much, don't leave me," she cried.

I'll spare the details of the rest of the time in bed. Suffice to say, I didn't get another pop at her, but as the afternoon rolled around, she had calmed down and accepted the way things were, no doubt a situation she'd been in before anyway, though probably without the upfront honesty.

As we were both finished packing, she stood dry-eyed with her back facing the window in her yellow shirt and jean shorts as the sun brightened up her beautiful golden hair. She was staring at me with a look of admiration and a smile, as if she was proud of me.

"You are a wonderful man."

There are many things to remember about that little sex excursion, but after returning home, it is that moment in the room packed up and ready to leave that Jenny gave me the only memory I relive every single day.

Epilogue

In case you are wondering, I did find Nicole in Manila for one last no-holds-barred session of sloppy sex. Condomless of course. And I did come home with chlamydia. I expect it was from that session as it didn't set in until almost two weeks after getting home, but I still told Jenny about it, which probably dampened her opinion of my wonderfulness. She said she got tested and didn't have it.

She didn't get pregnant either, and about four months later, she started posting pics on Facebook of a handsome 40-year-old Brit that she had fallen in love with. About six months after that, she was in England and a couple months after that, I was no longer her Facebook friend.

I struggled for a while with my decision of leaving her behind. I could have had her in the states with me to break up the excruciating daily grind. Who wouldn't struggle with that? It's possible to leave behind a girl such as Jenny when in the Philippines, but it seems absurd while working a 9-5 and eating microwave dinners alone in a western country.

Around that time, the president of the Philippines started a drug war, there were rampant murders in Manila, and I committed to taking my next sex excursion to Thailand. When I arrived in Pattaya, I patted myself on the back many times for breaking it off with Jenny so responsibly. Not only did it allow her to find what seemed like a great man to get her out of the Philippines, but it allowed me to fuck a ton more bargirls...

Or so I thought, perhaps it caused me more pain. More on that later.

FAQ

Where can I find more information on Angeles City and meeting girls?

Visit the author's website at SexExcursionist.com or try Google. There is near limitless information on traveling to sex destinations.

Why would you write a book like this?

For entertainment, sexual or otherwise. This is not meant as a how-to or why to become a sex tourist, though I included many of my thoughts on those subjects. While my own experiences may have felt more surreal than when they are put into words to be compared with all sex tourism experiences, I nevertheless felt it would make a good story. There is downtime on travels, so I wrote a book, please let me know what you thought of it!

Have the prices changed any?

Yes. Please visit the guides on SexExcursionist.com for more up-to-date information.

How much does a three week sex excursion to Angeles City cost?

If you are Allen, it can cost as little as $1,500USD, not including the plane ticket. For John, the sky is the limit, though it would be hard to spend more than $10,000 without ringing bells every night. For the average person looking to have a good time and stay in a decent hotel, while not worrying too much about pinching pennies, $200 per night is a good cushioned budget, so somewhere around $4,000 for a 3 week trip.

How much did you spend on this trip?

Around $8,000. $2,000 of which was spent spoiling Jenny.

The girls in this book seem to all want to marry you, is this a fabrication or are you a handsome guy?

No, and No. I'm exactly as I described in the first chapter, but I typically treat the girls much better than the average customer who treats them like a whore. In that respect, I often stand out. Regardless, Angeles City is not like a typical sex destination that men, in western countries especially, may think of. Most of the girls there are not forced into it due to drugs or mental health issues, for them, selling their body is a way to meet a husband and get paid for it in the process. Additionally, the time periods that are paid for are longer than with most prostitutes around the world. You don't pay for 30 minutes, you usually pay for a whole night, long enough to develop real feelings.

You really believe what those girls tell you?

Well, so many guys get hung up on whether or not the bargirls are telling them the truth, and I don't really understand it. I go on sex vacations for the fantasies, not to play the social game. That said, there are some relationships that can be formed with bargirls, even over a short period of time, that you can be fairly certain the emotions are genuine, whether or not the details she tells you of her life, her intentions, and her number of concurrent customers are truthful.

195

So, you really think you'll never marry a bargirl and bring her home?

Maybe when I'm 75.

Where can I meet Lynn (or Nicole or ...)?

You can't, she's not real. Though most of the characters in this book are based on actual bargirls and sex tourists that I met in Angeles City, the iteration of them that appears in this book would not be recognizable if you met who it was based on. Besides, during a visit to Angeles City, you should be able to do even better than any of the girls I've portrayed in this book.

Can we hang out on my next trip?

Not out of the question.

Would you prefer Angeles City or Pattaya?

Without question for a true Sex Excursionist, I'd prefer Angeles City. It's cheaper and the girls speak better English and in general are more passionate than their Thai counterparts.

If your vacation is more for beer and sunshine and would prefer not to have a conversation with the hole you stick your dick in, go for Pattaya.

Is the cover a real bargirl from Angeles City?

No. You will never find pics of real bargirls on any of the Sex Excursionist covers or web site, except in rare cases where they were paid for their modeling services.

Made in the USA
Coppell, TX
22 November 2020